# The Final Witness

Nya Luther King

Published by Poverty Eradication Trust ( Triple ISO ), 2025.

This is a work of fiction. Similarities to real people, places, or events are entirely coincidental.

THE FINAL WITNESS

**First edition. March 20, 2025.**

Copyright © 2025 Nya Luther King.

ISBN: 978-8198077936

Written by Nya Luther King.

# Table of Contents

Prologue .................................................................................. 1
Chapter 1: The Darkness Within ............................................ 3
Chapter 2: Shadows of Guilt .................................................. 7
Chapter 3: The Unraveling Threads ..................................... 11
Chapter 4: Hidden Agendas ................................................. 17
Chapter 5: Cracks in the Facade ........................................... 23
Chapter 6: Blood and Betrayal ............................................. 29
Chapter 7: Into the Abyss .................................................... 35
Chapter 8: Into the Serpent's Den ........................................ 41
Chapter 9: The Snare Tightens ............................................. 47
Chapter 10: Shadows and Alliances ..................................... 53
Chapter 11: Breaching the Fortress ...................................... 59
Chapter 12: The Calm Before the Storm ............................. 65
Chapter 13: The Reckoning ................................................. 71
Chapter 14: The Storm Before the Dawn ............................ 77
Chapter 15: Into the Shadows ............................................. 83
Chapter 16: A Game of Survival .......................................... 89
Chapter 17: After the Storm ................................................ 95
Chapter 18: The Calm Before the Storm ........................... 101
Chapter 19: The Confrontation ......................................... 107
Chapter 20: A New Dawn After the Battle ........................ 113
Chapter 21: The Investigation Deepens ............................. 117
Chapter 22: The Final Countdown .................................... 123
Chapter 23: A New Beginning ........................................... 127
Chapter 24: A Legacy of Courage ...................................... 129

*To the seekers of truth and the dreamers of justice.*

This book is for those who dare to face the shadows within and without, who believe that love can thrive even in the darkest of places, and who know that the human spirit is both fragile and unbreakable.

And to you, dear reader—because without your curiosity, courage, and heart, this story would never rise.

May it haunt your thoughts, ignite your passions, and remind you that every twist of fate holds the power to illuminate the truth.

*"The darkest truths are hidden in plain sight, waiting for the brave to uncover them. In the end, it's not the shadows we fear, but the light they might reveal."* —Dr. Raam Harvard

# Prologue

In the quiet town of Millwood, shadows lurked beneath the surface, masked by the idyllic facade of suburban life. It was a place where laughter echoed in the streets, where children played without a care, and neighbors exchanged friendly waves. Yet, beneath the warmth of the summer sun, darkness simmered, threatening to unravel the fabric of their community.

Eli Thompson stood at the edge of the local park, the familiar sights of his childhood now tinged with unease. The whispers of danger crept through the air, carried on the wind like a foreboding message. He felt it in his bones—the sensation of impending change, a storm brewing just beyond the horizon.

For months, rumors had spread like wildfire: strange figures moving in and out of abandoned buildings, late-night transactions in hidden corners, and the unmistakable scent of fear hanging heavy in the air. It was as if the innocence of their town was being traded away, one secret at a time.

Eli had always believed in the power of friendship and the strength found in unity. As summer drew to a close, he would soon discover just how fragile that belief could become when confronted with the harsh realities of the world. With his closest friends—Emma, Cole, and Carrie—by his side, he felt ready to face whatever darkness lay ahead.

But as the shadows grew longer and the sun dipped below the horizon, Eli couldn't shake the feeling that their lives were about to change forever. In a world where courage and fear would clash, he knew they would need to stand together, their voices rising against the encroaching silence.

Little did they know, the fight for their town had only just begun.

# Chapter 1: The Darkness Within

Detective Eli Marks sat at his desk, staring at the old photo pinned to the corner of his bulletin board. The edges were frayed, and the color had long since faded, but the image of Lily—his daughter, her soft smile, and wide brown eyes—remained etched into his mind. Two years. Two long years since she'd disappeared without a trace. The trail had gone cold, but the fire inside him never would.

He checked his watch—6:43 a.m. Another day, another case. He wasn't even supposed to be at the station this early, but sleep had become a luxury he could no longer afford. Not since that night. Not since the world had collapsed around him.

The precinct was eerily quiet, with only the hum of fluorescent lights breaking the silence. Eli leaned back in his chair, trying to shake off the weight pressing on his chest, but it never left. He had become a shell of his former self, though he wouldn't admit it. His colleagues tiptoed around him now, not daring to mention Lily's name. Except for Carrie, his partner. She understood him in a way no one else could, and though he wasn't sure how much longer he could hold it together, she was the only one who could still make him feel like a detective instead of a broken father.

"Marks, you in?" Carrie's voice rang out as she strolled into the room, her long brown coat swishing behind her. She always arrived with an air of purpose, like a storm gathering momentum. "We've got something big."

Eli straightened. "What is it?"

"Dead body. High profile. Judge Ethan Grayson," she said, tossing a file onto his desk. "Someone took him out in his own house last night."

Eli's stomach clenched. Judge Grayson was no ordinary target. He had presided over some of the city's most controversial cases, a hardliner against organized crime and corruption. His death wasn't just a murder—it was a statement.

"Do we have any suspects?" he asked, flipping through the file.

"Not yet," Carrie said, shrugging out of her coat and grabbing a cup of coffee from the break room. "But the forensics team is already there. His house is on lockdown. We're up."

Eli stood, his mind already racing. Grayson's murder wasn't a random act of violence; someone had wanted him dead. And that someone was likely part of the tangled web of criminals the judge had spent his career tearing apart. This wasn't going to be a simple investigation.

They rode in silence on the way to the judge's mansion. Eli stared out the window, the early morning light casting long shadows on the city streets. Everything felt darker these days, even when the sun was up. Carrie's fingers drummed on the steering wheel, her nervous energy filling the car.

"I heard Grayson had a lot of enemies," she said, breaking the silence.

"He wasn't exactly the most popular guy," Eli replied. "But going after a judge? That's gutsy, even for this city."

When they arrived at the mansion, the scene was already swarming with forensic techs and uniformed officers. The grand house loomed like a tombstone, its tall windows reflecting the grey morning sky. Crime scene tape stretched across the entrance, and the front door hung slightly ajar, as if the house itself was shocked by what had happened inside.

Eli and Carrie ducked under the tape and entered the house. The interior was cold and quiet, every surface polished to perfection. But as they stepped into the study, the air grew heavy with the scent of death. Judge Grayson sat slumped in his leather chair, a pool of dark blood staining the floor beneath him. His eyes were open, frozen in a final moment of terror.

Eli moved closer, his practiced eye scanning the room. The judge's desk was neat, save for a few scattered papers. No sign of a struggle. A clean, precise hit. Whoever did this knew exactly what they were doing.

"He was shot," Carrie said, examining the entry wound at the back of Grayson's skull. "Execution style."

"Professionals," Eli muttered. His gut tightened. The scene was too clean. Too controlled. This wasn't a spur-of-the-moment killing—it was planned, orchestrated.

Carrie pointed to the judge's desk. "What's that?"

A single photograph lay face down on the polished wood. Eli turned it over and felt a chill run down his spine. It was a picture of a girl—blonde, smiling, maybe sixteen. The name scribbled in the corner read *Lily*.

His hand trembled as he stared at the photo. No. It couldn't be.

"Eli..." Carrie's voice softened, but he couldn't hear her.

His mind raced, memories flooding back with every glance at the name. *Lily*. His Lily. But how? Why did Judge Grayson have a photo of his daughter? His heart pounded in his chest as he struggled to connect the dots. This murder had just become personal.

Carrie's hand touched his arm. "We need to stay focused, Eli. We'll figure this out."

Eli took a deep breath, nodding slowly. But deep down, a storm was already brewing. He wasn't just chasing a killer now—he was chasing the truth about what had happened to his daughter. And he was prepared to burn the whole city down to get it.

"Let's find out who did this," he said, his voice cold, determined.

Because whoever they were, they knew about Lily. And that made them dangerous.

# Chapter 2: Shadows of Guilt

Alice Graham paced in her office, her heels clicking on the polished hardwood floor. The early morning light filtered through the tall windows, casting long shadows across the sleek, modern furniture. She hated this office. It was too perfect, too sterile, a far cry from the messy, vibrant life she used to lead.

She couldn't shake the feeling that something was wrong. Her phone had buzzed twice already that morning, once with a call she didn't answer, and once with a text she couldn't ignore. A single line from an unknown number: **"We know what you did."**

Her hands trembled slightly as she scrolled back to the message, reading it again, as if it would somehow change. But it didn't. The words stayed the same, taunting her, reminding her that the past she thought she had buried was about to resurface.

"Damn it," she muttered under her breath, tossing her phone onto her desk. Her office assistant knocked softly on the door before peeking in.

"Ms. Graham, are you alright? You look pale."

"I'm fine, Sarah," Alice snapped, her voice sharper than she intended. "Just a busy morning."

"Okay, well, Mr. Lincoln is here to see you," Sarah said, her eyes flicking nervously toward the hallway.

Alice's stomach twisted. Of course, he was here. Marcus Lincoln was one of the most notorious crime lords in the city, a man with enough power and influence to make anyone disappear. And she had represented him in court—more than once.

Alice forced a smile, though the tension in her body betrayed her. "Send him in."

Marcus Lincoln sauntered into the room like he owned the place, his dark suit tailored to perfection. His presence filled the space, radiating confidence and danger. He was in his late fifties, his hair graying at the temples, but his eyes were sharp and cold, like a predator sizing up its prey.

"Alice," he said, his voice smooth and low. "You don't look well. Everything alright?"

She bristled at his tone. He always had a way of knowing when something was wrong, like he could smell fear. Alice had spent years building a reputation as one of the best defense attorneys in the city—ruthless, relentless, and unbeatable. But Marcus Lincoln was a reminder that no matter how high you climbed, there were always strings attached. And he was holding one of them.

"Everything's fine," she lied. "I assume you're not here just to check on my health."

Lincoln smiled, but it didn't reach his eyes. "You're right. I'm here because I need a favor. I'm sure you've heard the news by now. Judge Grayson is dead."

Alice felt her heart skip a beat. Grayson? Dead?

"I've heard," she said, keeping her voice steady. "But what does that have to do with me?"

Lincoln sat down in the chair across from her desk, crossing his legs casually. "Grayson was involved in a lot of things—things that are bad for business. He had files, Alice. Files on people like me, on people like you."

Her pulse quickened. Files on her? That couldn't be possible. She had always been careful, always made sure to cover her tracks. But if what Lincoln was saying was true...

"I don't know what you're talking about," Alice said, but the words felt hollow even to her.

"Don't play coy," Lincoln said, his voice dropping a notch. "You represented me more than once, Alice. You've seen the kind of things I deal with. If those files get into the wrong hands, we're all screwed. So, I need you to make sure they don't."

Alice's mind raced. Grayson's murder was already making waves through the legal and criminal underworld. But this? This was something bigger. If Lincoln was telling the truth, someone out there had dangerous information, and they wouldn't hesitate to use it.

"I'm not in the business of destroying evidence," Alice said, though she knew she was already entangled in this. She had been for years. "What exactly do you want me to do?"

Lincoln leaned forward, his eyes narrowing. "I want you to find out who has those files and get them back. Before the cops do. Before anyone else does."

Alice felt a cold sweat prick the back of her neck. This wasn't just about saving Lincoln. It was about saving herself. If Grayson had something on her—something that could connect her to the things she had done—her career, her freedom, her life, all of it was at risk.

"I don't have the resources for something like that," she said carefully. "I'm not an investigator."

"No," Lincoln said, standing up slowly. "But you're smart. And you've got a lot to lose if this gets out."

He didn't need to elaborate. Alice knew exactly what he meant. She had made deals, taken risks, and crossed lines she couldn't uncross. And now, it was all catching up to her.

Lincoln paused at the door, turning to give her one last look. "I'd hate for anything to happen to that beautiful daughter of yours, Alice. Such a bright future ahead of her."

Her blood turned to ice. Sophie. The thought of her daughter being dragged into this nightmare made Alice's head spin. Lincoln had never directly threatened Sophie before, but his veiled words were enough. Alice knew what kind of man he was. And if she didn't play by his rules, Sophie would become collateral damage.

As soon as the door closed behind him, Alice collapsed into her chair, burying her face in her hands. She needed to think, to figure out her next move. But her mind was racing, spinning out of control. The files. Grayson's death. Lincoln's threat. It was all spiraling too fast.

Her phone buzzed again, cutting through her thoughts. With shaking hands, she picked it up and saw another message from the unknown number.

**"You've been warned. Your daughter is next."**

Alice's breath caught in her throat. Whoever was behind this knew everything. They knew about her, about Sophie, about what she had done. And they weren't going to stop.

She had no choice now. She would have to find those files. Because if she didn't, the past wasn't just going to catch up with her—it was going to destroy her.

Her fingers hovered over her phone for a moment before she dialed the number she never thought she'd need again. The phone rang twice before a familiar voice answered.

"Alice?" the voice said, wary.

"It's me, Eli," she whispered, her voice shaking. "I need your help."

# Chapter 3: The Unraveling Threads

Detective Eli Marks leaned against his car, staring at the entrance to Judge Grayson's mansion, still processing the image of his daughter's photo found on the dead man's desk. His gut churned with questions he couldn't answer. Why was Lily's picture there? What connection did she have to Grayson? And how was any of this tied to her disappearance?

The crime scene was busy, filled with forensics officers and cops going about their business, but for Eli, time seemed to have frozen. His mind kept returning to that moment—the picture, the name. *Lily.* Two years, and he was no closer to finding her. Now, this? He wasn't sure if it was a clue or another cruel twist of fate.

Carrie stood next to him, hands shoved deep into her pockets, watching the flurry of activity around them. She had noticed the shift in Eli's demeanor the moment he had seen the photograph, and while she didn't say anything, she knew exactly what it meant to him.

"We're not letting this one go, Eli," she said quietly, her voice cutting through the fog in his mind. "We'll get to the bottom of it. Grayson's death... it's connected to something bigger."

Eli nodded, but his thoughts were elsewhere. He needed to stay focused on the case, but with every passing second, his instincts screamed that this was personal. It wasn't just about Judge Grayson's murder anymore—it was about Lily. And if someone had killed the judge to bury whatever secrets he was keeping, Eli wouldn't stop until he unearthed every last one of them.

His phone buzzed in his pocket, breaking him out of his reverie. He fished it out, glancing at the screen. A name flashed across it: *Alice Graham.*

He hesitated for a moment, memories flooding back of the last time he had spoken to Alice. They hadn't parted on good terms. She had always lived on the edge of the law, representing the kind of clients Eli spent his life trying to put away. But there was history between them, a complicated web of professional rivalry and unspoken understanding. And now, she was calling him.

Carrie raised an eyebrow as he answered the call. "Alice?"

Her voice came through shaky, a far cry from her usual confident tone. "Eli. I need your help."

Eli straightened, his muscles tensing. Alice wasn't the type to ask for help—especially from him. If she was calling, it meant something was seriously wrong.

"What's going on?" he asked, his eyes narrowing.

There was a pause on the other end, a hesitation that was unusual for Alice. "I... can't talk over the phone. It's complicated."

Eli glanced at Carrie, who was listening closely. "Alice, if this is about one of your clients—"

"It's not," she interrupted, her voice sharper now. "It's about me. And Judge Grayson."

Eli's heart skipped a beat. Grayson? Alice was mixed up in this? He motioned for Carrie to follow him, and they walked to the edge of the property, away from prying ears.

"Meet me at my office in an hour," Alice continued, her voice low. "And Eli—be careful. We're not the only ones looking into this."

Before he could respond, the line went dead.

Carrie crossed her arms, her eyes fixed on him. "What did she say?"

"Alice is involved," Eli said, slipping the phone back into his pocket. "She didn't give details, but she's connected to Grayson somehow. Said she needs to talk in person."

Carrie's brow furrowed. "Alice Graham? You think she's a suspect?"

"I don't know," Eli admitted. "But if she's calling me, it means something's rattled her. And Alice doesn't rattle easily."

Carrie glanced back at the mansion. "Grayson was a high-profile target. If Alice is involved, it could mean her clients were, too. The kind of clients who make people disappear."

"Exactly," Eli muttered. He had a sinking feeling in his gut that this case was about to get a whole lot messier.

**Alice's Office – One Hour Later**

Eli and Carrie arrived at Alice's office just as the sun began to rise higher in the sky, casting long shadows across the city. The office was a sleek glass structure downtown, an expensive testament to Alice's success as a defense attorney. She had built a reputation for taking on the cases no one else wanted, and it had made her both feared and admired in equal measure.

As they stepped inside, Alice's assistant, Sarah, nervously waved them in. Eli could tell by the tension in the room that whatever was going on, it had the entire office on edge.

"Alice is in her office," Sarah said, her voice barely above a whisper.

They made their way down the hall and knocked on the door. Alice's voice called out, "Come in."

Eli pushed open the door, stepping into themalist, high-end office. Alice stood by the window, staring out at the city, her back to them. She turned when they entered, and Eli could see the exhaustion etched into her features. Her usually pristine appearance was a little disheveled, her blouse slightly wrinkled, her hair pulled back hastily.

"Alice," Eli said, crossing the room. "What's going on?"

She didn't answer right away, instead motioning for them to sit. Carrie eyed Alice with suspicion as she took a seat next to Eli.

"I'll cut to the chase," Alice said, her voice low, almost strained. "Someone's trying to frame me for Judge Grayson's murder."

Eli exchanged a look with Carrie. "Frame you?"

Alice nodded, her eyes hard. "Yesterday, I received an envelope—anonymous. Inside, there was evidence linking me to Grayson's death. A picture of me at his house from two nights ago, some forged documents, even a red coat that supposedly matches the one seen leaving the crime scene."

Eli leaned forward. "Why were you at his house?"

Alice hesitated, then sighed. "I went to see him about a case—something from years ago. Grayson was involved in an old investigation, and I needed his help... but now, whoever killed him is trying to pin it on me."

Carrie crossed her arms, skeptical. "And why should we believe you?"

Alice's eyes flashed with anger. "I know I'm not the cleanest attorney in this city, but I didn't kill him. And I didn't have a reason to."

Eli studied her closely, searching for any signs of deceit. But beneath the anger and fear, he saw something else—genuine desperation.

"Who would want to frame you?" he asked.

Alice looked away, her voice barely a whisper. "Marcus Lincoln."

Carrie's expression darkened. "Lincoln? The crime lord?"

Eli felt the air in the room grow heavier. If Marcus Lincoln was involved, things were worse than he had imagined. Lincoln was untouchable, always a step ahead of the law. And if he wanted Alice framed, there was no telling how deep this went.

"I represented him years ago," Alice explained, her voice faltering. "I know things... things that could destroy him. But I never crossed him, Eli. I swear."

Eli clenched his jaw, his mind racing. This wasn't just about Grayson's murder anymore. Lincoln, the files, Lily—it was all connected. And now Alice was caught in the crossfire.

"If Lincoln's involved, you're in serious danger," Eli said. "We need to figure out what he's hiding. Why kill Grayson now? What's in those files?"

Alice's eyes met his, fear clouding them. "I don't know. But if we don't find out soon, we're all going to be buried with Grayson."

Eli stood, his resolve hardening. He had come here for answers, and now he had more questions than ever. But one thing was clear—this case was bigger than he could have imagined. And somewhere in this tangled web of lies, his daughter's fate was tied to it all.

"We're going to find out the truth," he said, locking eyes with Alice. "And we're going to take Lincoln down."

But deep down, Eli knew the clock was ticking. And the longer they waited, the closer the shadows crept toward them all.

# Chapter 4: Hidden Agendas

The air was thick with tension as Eli and Carrie left Alice's office. The city outside hummed with life, oblivious to the dark, dangerous undercurrents lurking beneath the surface. Eli's thoughts churned with every step they took toward the car. Marcus Lincoln. A criminal mastermind with enough power to manipulate the system and enough cruelty to crush anyone who stood in his way.

Eli's hand tightened on the car door handle as he glanced at Carrie. She was silent, her brows furrowed in deep thought. They had tangled with powerful people before, but Lincoln was different. He was a puppet master, and if Alice was right, he was pulling the strings behind Grayson's murder. But why?

"We need to find out more about those files," Carrie said, breaking the silence as they got into the car. "Grayson was keeping something on Lincoln—and maybe others. If that's what got him killed, we're dealing with more than just a hit. This could be a full-blown cover-up."

Eli nodded, though his mind was only half on the case. His thoughts kept circling back to the photo of Lily. What if she was a part of this puzzle? What if Grayson had known something about her disappearance, and that's why he had her picture?

"We need a starting point," Carrie continued. "Alice was too vague. Do you think she's holding back?"

"Definitely," Eli replied, starting the engine. "But she's scared. Alice doesn't rattle easily, but Lincoln's got her shaken. We need to figure out what's in those files and who else might want them."

Carrie stared out the window as they drove, her voice thoughtful. "Do you think it's possible... that Lily's tied to this somehow?"

Eli's grip tightened on the steering wheel. He didn't want to admit it, but it was exactly what he feared. "I don't know," he said slowly, his voice strained. "But if Grayson had something on Lily, it changes everything."

Carrie didn't push further, sensing Eli's unease. "We could dig into Grayson's old cases," she suggested. "Maybe something from his past connects to Lily or Lincoln. It's a long shot, but it might give us a lead."

Eli nodded again, his jaw clenched. They needed to approach this methodically, but every instinct in him was screaming to tear through the city, demanding answers about Lily. He forced himself to stay focused. Grayson's files were key, and whoever had them was still out there—possibly connected to Lincoln, possibly holding the answers to both Grayson's murder and Lily's disappearance.

## THE PRECINCT – EARLY Afternoon

Back at the precinct, Eli and Carrie sat across from Detective Frank Donnelly, the lead investigator from the forensics unit. Frank was a stout man with graying hair and a deep, no-nonsense frown that seemed permanently etched into his face. His team had just finished processing the evidence from Grayson's mansion.

"What've you got for us, Frank?" Carrie asked, leaning forward.

Frank slid a file across the table. "It's not much, but it's something. Grayson's office was wiped clean, which means whoever killed him didn't want us to find anything. But we pulled a partial print off the desk—someone touched that photo of the girl."

Eli's pulse quickened. "You get a match?"

Frank nodded grimly. "Came back to a known associate of Marcus Lincoln. Name's Nico Ramirez. Small-time thug who graduated to running dirty errands for Lincoln's organization. We've had him on our radar, but never had enough to pin anything major on him."

Carrie's eyes flicked to Eli. "That's not a coincidence."

"No," Eli agreed. "If Ramirez was there, Lincoln's involved. But what was Ramirez doing with a picture of my daughter?"

Frank sighed. "That's the other thing. The photo—it wasn't a recent one. We looked into it. The picture was taken from an old file. The date on the back puts it at least two years ago."

Eli's heart sank. *Two years.* Right around the time Lily disappeared. He could feel Carrie's eyes on him, but he couldn't meet her gaze. The weight of this revelation crashed over him like a wave. Ramirez had something to do with Lily. And if Lincoln was pulling Ramirez's strings, then Lincoln knew something about her disappearance.

"I need to talk to Ramirez," Eli said, standing abruptly.

"We don't know where he is," Frank said quickly. "Ramirez vanished off the grid right after Grayson's murder. Lincoln's probably hiding him."

"Then we'll find Lincoln," Eli snapped, his frustration boiling over. "We need to push harder. Ramirez knows something—about Grayson, about the files, and about Lily."

Carrie stood up next to him. "We'll track him down. But we need to be smart about it. Lincoln's got connections everywhere. We don't want to alert him that we're closing in."

Eli knew she was right, but his patience was wearing thin. Every second that passed was a second wasted, and he couldn't shake the fear gnawing at his chest—that Lily was out there somewhere, caught in the middle of a deadly game he barely understood.

**Marcus Lincoln's Private Club – Late Afternoon**

The front of *The Silver Lotus*, Marcus Lincoln's exclusive club, was unassuming—a sleek, glassy facade tucked between skyscrapers downtown. But behind those doors was a different world, where Lincoln conducted business with a select few, hidden from the public eye. Eli had never set foot in the place, but he knew its reputation. Deals were made here, secrets were bought and sold, and enemies were destroyed without ever setting foot in a courtroom.

Carrie and Eli stood outside, casing the entrance from across the street. Eli's heart pounded with a mixture of rage and determination. He wasn't supposed to go after Lincoln directly—protocol demanded more care—but Eli had never been one for protocol, not when it came to his daughter.

"You sure about this?" Carrie asked, her voice low. "We don't have a warrant, and Lincoln's too well-connected to just barge in on."

Eli's jaw tightened. "We're not here to make an arrest. We're here to send a message. If Lincoln's involved in Lily's disappearance, I want him to know we're coming for him."

Carrie gave him a cautious look but nodded. "Let's do it."

They crossed the street and approached the entrance. The doorman, a hulking figure in a black suit, eyed them suspiciously as they walked up.

"Members only," he said, blocking their path.

Eli flashed his badge. "We're not here to join. We're here to see Marcus Lincoln."

The doorman's eyes flicked between Eli and Carrie, lingering on the badge before narrowing. "Mr. Lincoln isn't available."

"Make him available," Eli growled, his voice cold.

The doorman smirked. "You don't just walk in here, Detective. Mr. Lincoln has friends in high places. You want to talk to him, you better come with something more than—"

Before he could finish, Eli grabbed him by the collar and shoved him against the wall. The smirk vanished from the man's face, replaced by shock.

"Listen carefully," Eli said, his voice a low growl. "I don't care about your rules or Lincoln's friends. I care about my daughter. And if Lincoln knows something, you better believe I'll burn this place to the ground to get to him."

Carrie stepped forward, placing a hand on Eli's arm, a silent warning to pull back. The doorman's eyes flickered with fear, but he held his ground.

"You're making a mistake," the doorman muttered. "You're in over your head."

Eli leaned in closer, his face inches from the man's. "Tell Lincoln I'm coming for him. And he can't hide forever."

With that, he released the man, who staggered back, adjusting his suit with a trembling hand.

Carrie shot Eli a look as they turned and walked away. "You think that'll scare Lincoln?"

"No," Eli said, his voice dark. "But it'll make him nervous. And right now, that's all we need."

As they walked down the street, the weight of what they were facing settled deeper in Eli's gut. Lincoln wasn't the type to back down, and Eli had just declared war. But he didn't care. Somewhere in this twisted web of lies and murder was the truth about Lily.

And nothing would stop him from finding it.

# Chapter 5: Cracks in the Facade

Alice sat in her office, hands trembling around a glass of whiskey. She had barely touched it, but the glass still felt cold in her hands, as if holding onto it would keep her grounded. The walls seemed to close in on her. She was a master at staying composed under pressure—years of defending criminals had taught her that. But this was different. This time, *she* was the one under attack.

The message on her phone played over and over in her mind: **"You've been warned. Your daughter is next."**

Sophie.

Alice squeezed her eyes shut, trying to block out the panic rising in her chest. She had done everything to keep Sophie out of this life, to keep her safe. But now, the walls she had so carefully built were crumbling.

Her office door creaked open, and Sarah, her assistant, peered in nervously. "Ms. Graham, are you alright? You haven't taken any meetings today."

"I'm fine, Sarah," Alice said, forcing a smile she didn't feel. "I just need some time to think."

Sarah hesitated, her brow furrowed with concern. "I've—uh—heard some things. People are talking about Judge Grayson's death. Some of your clients... they've been asking questions. About you."

Alice's stomach churned. It wasn't just Marcus Lincoln she had to worry about. Her name was being whispered in the shadows, and soon enough, people would start looking for someone to blame.

"Don't worry about it," Alice said, her voice sharper than she intended. "It'll blow over. Just keep doing your job."

Sarah nodded, though the uncertainty in her eyes lingered. As she left, Alice exhaled shakily, her mind spinning. She couldn't stay still—waiting for the hammer to drop wasn't an option.

With a sudden surge of determination, she grabbed her phone and dialed the only number she knew could help her now.

**Eli's Apartment – Late Evening**

Eli stood by the window, staring out at the city. The lights blinked in the distance, casting long shadows across the room. He hadn't heard from Alice since their tense meeting earlier, and something told him that she was in deeper trouble than she was letting on.

His phone buzzed on the table behind him, startling him from his thoughts. He glanced at the screen: *Alice Graham*.

For a split second, he debated not answering. But he couldn't afford to ignore her, not when they were both caught in the same storm. He picked up the phone.

"Alice."

"I need to meet," her voice came through tight, controlled. But Eli could hear the fear behind it. "Tonight."

Eli frowned. "Why? What's going on?"

There was a long pause before Alice responded. "I think... I think I'm being followed. They're watching me."

Eli's heart quickened. "Where are you?"

"I'm at my office," she said, her voice barely above a whisper. "I need your help, Eli. I can't keep running from this."

Eli didn't hesitate. "I'm on my way."

**ALICE'S OFFICE – NIGHT**

The building was quiet when Eli arrived, the once-bustling offices now dark, save for the faint glow of Alice's office window on the top floor. He made his way up the empty elevator, the tension in his body tightening with each floor.

When the doors opened, Alice was already waiting for him, standing just inside the entrance to her office. Her face was pale, her usually sharp features softened by exhaustion and fear.

"Thanks for coming," she said, her voice barely above a whisper as she closed the door behind him.

Eli didn't waste any time. "Who's following you? Do you know?"

Alice shook her head, pacing the room. "I don't know, but it's not just Lincoln. I think… I think someone else wants those files too. Grayson had a lot of enemies, Eli. And now, whoever they are, they think I have something that could ruin them."

Eli studied her, seeing the cracks in her usual armor. This wasn't the confident, cold attorney he was used to. This was someone who was genuinely afraid—for herself, and for Sophie.

"Tell me everything," Eli said, his voice steady. "Don't hold back. What do you know about those files? And why are they so important?"

Alice stopped pacing and looked at him, her eyes filled with a mixture of guilt and desperation. "I don't have the files," she admitted. "But I know what's in them. Grayson… he kept records on everyone. Judges, politicians, criminals. He knew who was on Lincoln's payroll, who was dirty, who could be blackmailed. He had enough leverage to control half the city."

Eli's mind raced. "And now that Grayson's dead, everyone's scrambling to get their hands on those records."

Alice nodded. "Lincoln's desperate to keep them from falling into the wrong hands. But there's someone else—someone who's willing to kill to get them first."

Eli's thoughts flickered to Ramirez, the thug connected to Lincoln, and the picture of Lily. "Does this have anything to do with Lily? Why was her picture in Grayson's office?"

Alice bit her lip, her eyes flickering with guilt. "I don't know," she said, her voice barely audible. "But Eli, if Grayson had something on your daughter... you're not the only one who's been looking for her."

Eli felt a cold chill run down his spine. He had suspected as much, but hearing it confirmed sent a fresh wave of dread through him.

"Why didn't you tell me earlier?" he demanded, his voice tight with anger. "If you knew something about Lily—"

"I didn't know for sure," Alice said quickly, her voice cracking. "I thought it was a coincidence. I didn't want to drag you into this unless I had proof."

Eli took a step back, running a hand through his hair. He wanted to be angry with her, but he knew this wasn't just about Alice hiding information—it was about survival. They were both in over their heads, and now, the clock was ticking faster than ever.

"What do we do now?" Alice asked, her voice shaky. "I can't keep running from Lincoln. If I don't find those files, he'll kill me—and worse, he'll come after Sophie."

Eli clenched his fists, the weight of the situation pressing down on him. He couldn't let that happen. Not to Alice, and not to Sophie.

"We're going to find those files," he said, his voice resolute. "But we're going to do it on our terms. No more running."

Alice nodded, though the fear in her eyes remained.

Eli pulled out his phone and dialed Carrie's number. She picked up on the first ring.

"We need to move," Eli said without preamble. "Grayson's files are the key to everything. We need to track down Ramirez—he's the link between Lincoln and those files."

"I've been working on that," Carrie replied. "I found a lead on Ramirez's last known location. I'll send you the address."

Eli hung up and turned back to Alice. "Stay here. Lock your doors, and don't leave until I call you. If anyone tries to come after you, call me."

Alice nodded, her face pale but determined. "Be careful, Eli."

He gave her a reassuring nod before stepping out of her office, his mind racing. They were close, but so was Lincoln. And somewhere in the shadows, the truth about Lily—and Grayson's files—was waiting to be uncovered.

**Ramirez's Hideout – Midnight**

Eli and Carrie pulled up outside an old, dilapidated warehouse on the outskirts of the city. The building was abandoned, its windows boarded up, but there was a single light on inside. Ramirez had gone to ground, and this was where he was hiding.

Carrie checked her gun as they stepped out of the car. "We go in quiet," she said. "We don't know how many people Lincoln has watching this place."

Eli nodded, his focus sharpened. "We need Ramirez alive. He's the only one who knows where the files are."

They moved quickly and silently, their footsteps barely audible on the gravel as they approached the warehouse. Eli could feel the tension in the air, the sense that they were walking into something dangerous, something bigger than they could see.

As they reached the door, Carrie gave him a nod, and Eli kicked it open in one swift motion.

The inside of the warehouse was dimly lit, the flickering light casting eerie shadows across the room. Ramirez was there, sitting at a table, a gun in front of him.

He looked up, startled, his eyes widening in fear when he saw them. "Wait—wait! I didn't do anything!"

Eli and Carrie moved in quickly, their guns trained on Ramirez.

"Where are the files?" Eli demanded, his voice cold.

Ramirez's hands shook as he held them up. "I don't have them! I swear!"

"Liar," Carrie hissed, stepping forward. "You were at Grayson's house. You touched that photo. You know something."

"I— I was hired!" Ramirez stammered, backing away. "Lincoln told me to retrieve something from Grayson's office after he was killed. But when I got there, it was gone. Someone else took it!"

Eli's heart pounded. "Who?"

Ramirez shook his head frantically. "I don't know!"

# Chapter 6: Blood and Betrayal

The warehouse felt suffocating, the air thick with the weight of unanswered questions and half-truths. Ramirez stood with his back against the wall, his face drenched in sweat, fear written in every nervous twitch of his hands. Eli's grip on his gun remained steady, though inside, his blood simmered with impatience.

"Who took the files, Ramirez?" Eli growled, taking a step closer. "You know something. Lincoln sent you to Grayson's office for a reason."

Ramirez's wide eyes darted between Eli and Carrie, panic rising in his chest. "I swear, I don't know!" he cried, voice cracking. "When I got there, the safe was already open. The files—whatever they were—they were gone. But Lincoln, he thinks I'm lying. He's going to kill me!"

"Then why don't you tell us the truth before he gets the chance?" Carrie said, her voice sharp. "You had something to do with this, Ramirez. You don't just break into a dead man's house for a joyride."

Ramirez swallowed hard, his breath ragged. "I didn't kill Grayson," he said, voice trembling. "I just followed orders. Lincoln wanted those files—he wanted leverage on everyone Grayson had dirt on. But there was someone else there that night. I saw them leave right before I got inside."

Eli's eyes narrowed. "Who?"

"I didn't get a good look, but it wasn't one of Lincoln's guys. It was a woman," Ramirez muttered. "I saw her silhouette as she ran. Blonde, I think. She got there first."

A cold chill crept up Eli's spine. His mind raced back to Alice. Could she have been involved somehow? Was there something she hadn't told him? He shook off the thought, but it lingered in the back of his mind like a shadow.

"Where did she go?" Carrie pressed. "Did you follow her?"

Ramirez shook his head frantically. "No. I went straight for the safe. I thought she had left the files behind, but they were already gone. I tried to call Lincoln, but I panicked. That's when I bolted."

Eli and Carrie exchanged a glance. A woman—someone who knew Grayson's secrets—had beaten Ramirez to the files. And if Ramirez wasn't lying, that woman could be their only link to uncovering what was really going on.

"Lincoln's going to kill me," Ramirez said again, his voice quivering. "You don't understand. He's ruthless. If he thinks I double-crossed him—"

"He won't get the chance if you help us," Eli interrupted, his voice steely. "You're going to tell us everything you know about Lincoln's operation. Every name, every deal. You give us enough, and we'll make sure he doesn't touch you."

Ramirez hesitated, eyes flicking nervously between Eli and the door. "I—"

A sudden crash shattered the silence, and the warehouse door burst open with a violent bang. Before anyone could react, gunfire erupted from the entrance, bullets tearing through the air with deafening intensity.

Eli and Carrie dove behind a stack of crates as the shots ricocheted off the concrete walls. Ramirez screamed, diving for cover, but he was too slow. A single shot caught him in the shoulder, spinning him to the ground with a cry of pain.

"Get down!" Eli shouted to Carrie as more gunmen flooded into the warehouse, their faces masked and their weapons drawn. Lincoln's men. They had found Ramirez, and now they were cleaning up.

Carrie popped up from behind the crates, firing off two rounds, hitting one of the gunmen square in the chest. He collapsed to the ground with a grunt, but more kept coming, their boots echoing ominously against the concrete floor.

"We're pinned!" Carrie shouted over the gunfire, ducking back behind the crates.

Eli's mind raced as he scanned the room. There were at least four more shooters, and they were closing in fast. Ramirez was bleeding out on the floor, writhing in pain, but if they didn't move soon, none of them would get out alive.

"We need to get Ramirez out of here," Eli said, his voice low and urgent. "He's no good to us dead."

Carrie nodded, reloading her weapon with quick precision. "Cover me."

Eli sprang to his feet, unleashing a flurry of gunfire at the approaching men, forcing them to scatter behind cover. Carrie moved swiftly, grabbing Ramirez by the collar and dragging him behind the crates as he groaned in agony.

"They'll cut us off at the exits," Carrie said, breathing heavily. "We need to find another way out."

Eli's eyes flickered to a small side door on the far end of the warehouse. It was their only chance. "There," he pointed. "We can get out through there, but we need to move now."

Carrie glanced at the door, then nodded. "Let's go."

She hoisted Ramirez to his feet, keeping him upright as they made their way toward the exit, ducking and weaving between the crates. The gunfire grew louder, closer. One of Lincoln's men shouted something Eli couldn't make out over the chaos, but the meaning was clear: they were closing in.

Just as they reached the door, a figure appeared from the shadows, blocking their path. It was one of Lincoln's top enforcers, a massive man with cold, dark eyes and a deadly calm about him. He raised his gun, and for a brief, terrifying moment, Eli thought they were finished.

But before the man could fire, a single gunshot rang out from the far side of the room. The enforcer staggered, his gun dropping to the floor as he clutched his bleeding side. Carrie wasted no time, firing two more shots into his chest, dropping him to the ground.

"Move!" Eli shouted, throwing open the side door. They stumbled out into the cold night air, the sounds of the warehouse fading behind them as they ran toward their car. Ramirez was barely conscious, his face pale from the blood loss, but he was still alive.

Carrie shoved him into the backseat as Eli jumped into the driver's seat, slamming the car into gear and tearing down the street. The adrenaline surged through his veins, his knuckles white on the steering wheel.

"That was too close," Carrie said, breathing heavily, her eyes scanning the rearview mirror for any sign of pursuit.

Eli nodded, his jaw clenched. They had barely made it out, and they were no closer to finding the files—or Lily.

"We need answers, Ramirez," Eli said, his voice cold as he glanced at the wounded man in the backseat. "Who was that woman? What's Lincoln planning?"

Ramirez coughed, blood staining his shirt. "I... I don't know," he wheezed. "But... but I know where she is."

Eli's heart skipped a beat. "Where?"

Ramirez's eyes fluttered, struggling to stay conscious. "There's... there's a place," he rasped. "An old safehouse... Lincoln used it to stash things. She'll be there... looking for the rest of the files."

Eli exchanged a glance with Carrie. They finally had a lead, but it came with a heavy price. Ramirez was fading fast, and if they didn't act quickly, he might not live to give them anything more.

"We'll get you to a hospital," Eli said, pressing the gas pedal harder. "But if you're lying, Ramirez—if you're leading us into a trap—I'll make sure Lincoln isn't your biggest problem."

Ramirez didn't respond, his head slumping back against the seat as his breathing grew shallow.

Carrie glanced at Eli, her expression grim. "We're running out of time."

Eli nodded, his thoughts racing. Lincoln was closing in, the files were still out there, and now a mystery woman was caught in the middle of it all. And behind everything, the looming question of Lily remained, gnawing at him with every passing second.

He had sworn to find the truth, no matter what. But with every step they took, the darkness seemed to grow deeper, the shadows longer.

And Eli knew—before this was over—more blood would be spilled.

**Marcus Lincoln's Estate – Midnight**

Marcus Lincoln sat in his office, the dim light casting long shadows across his face. His phone buzzed, and he glanced at the screen, his expression darkening.

The message was short, but it was enough.

**"Ramirez is alive. And they're coming for you."**

Lincoln's lips curled into a grim smile. "Let them come."

He leaned back in his chair, steepling his fingers as he stared out the window into the night. This game had only just begun.

And Eli Shepherd had no idea what he was walking into.

## Chapter 7: Into the Abyss

The hospital waiting room buzzed with quiet murmurs, the kind of subdued energy that comes with too many lives hanging by a thread. Eli stood near the window, staring out into the dark cityscape. Ramirez was in surgery, his chances slim. Carrie sat on the edge of a chair, tapping her fingers anxiously on her knee.

Neither of them had spoken much since their narrow escape from the warehouse. Eli's mind was racing, piecing together the fragments of information Ramirez had given them.

**An old safehouse. The woman. The files.**

It wasn't enough. They were chasing shadows, and every step deeper into the darkness put them closer to Lincoln's crosshairs.

Carrie broke the silence. "You think Ramirez will make it?"

Eli didn't look at her, his jaw tight. "Does it matter? We can't wait for him. We need to move on that safehouse lead."

Carrie sighed, rubbing her temple. "And if it's a trap? We're not exactly swimming in options here, Eli. We got out by the skin of our teeth last time."

Eli finally turned, his eyes hard. "We don't have a choice. Lincoln won't stop until he finds those files—and whoever that woman is, she's got answers. If she's there, we need to find her first."

Carrie met his gaze, nodding slowly. "Alright. But if this goes south, we'll need more than just our guns. We need backup, or at least a way to even the odds."

Eli ran a hand through his hair, exhaling deeply. "I know a guy—someone who owes me. He's off the grid, ex-military. We'll need his help for this."

Carrie raised an eyebrow. "Sounds like a story."

Eli shook his head. "Not one worth telling. Let's just say he knows how to disappear. And if we're going into Lincoln's world, disappearing might be our best bet."

Carrie smirked, standing up. "Lead the way then. But if this friend of yours is as shady as he sounds, I'm going to want some extra firepower."

**Eastside Bar – 2:00 AM**

The dimly lit dive bar was tucked away in a forgotten corner of the city, a place where people went to be invisible. The bartender didn't ask questions, and the patrons kept their eyes down. Eli walked through the door, scanning the room until his eyes landed on a man sitting alone at the far end of the bar.

He was tall, broad-shouldered, with a military haircut that hadn't quite grown out. His face was hardened, but not from age—it was the look of someone who had seen too much and done too many things that couldn't be undone.

Eli approached, and the man glanced up, his expression neutral. "Eli Shepherd. Didn't think I'd ever see you again."

"Didn't think I'd have to call in that favor, Cole," Eli said, sitting down next to him.

Cole leaned back in his chair, studying Eli. "You've got that look about you—the one that says you're neck-deep in something dangerous."

Eli didn't bother denying it. "I need your help. A job, and it's not clean."

Cole smirked. "It never is with you, is it?"

Eli nodded toward Carrie, who had stationed herself at the bar, watching their backs. "We're up against Marcus Lincoln. You've heard the name."

Cole's face darkened. "Lincoln? You really know how to pick your enemies."

"Yeah, well, we don't have time to be picky," Eli said. "I need someone who can handle themselves in a firefight and stay off the grid. We're going to a place that might get messy."

Cole was quiet for a long moment, then he nodded slowly. "I'll help. But this makes us square, Shepherd. After this, you're on your own."

"Fair enough," Eli replied. "We leave in an hour. Bring what you need."

Cole glanced at his glass, then downed the last of his drink. "Guess I'm back in the game."

**The Safehouse – 4:30 AM**

The safehouse was a crumbling old factory on the edge of the city, long abandoned and forgotten. Graffiti covered the rusted walls, and broken windows stared out like empty eyes. It was the perfect place to hide something—or someone—important.

Eli parked the car a few blocks away, the three of them moving in silence through the shadows. Carrie held her gun ready, eyes scanning the surroundings for any signs of movement. Cole moved with the quiet precision of a trained soldier, his senses alert for any threats.

They reached the side entrance, a rusted metal door barely hanging on its hinges. Eli motioned for Carrie and Cole to take position, then slowly pushed the door open. It creaked loudly, echoing through the empty halls.

The inside was just as decayed as the outside—dust-covered floors, collapsed beams, and stacks of forgotten crates. The air smelled of rust and neglect.

They moved through the building cautiously, their footsteps barely making a sound. Every creak of the floorboards, every distant noise, set Eli's nerves on edge. Somewhere in this maze of decay, the woman who had beaten Ramirez to the files was waiting.

Or maybe something worse.

As they turned a corner, they heard it—voices. Low, muffled, coming from deeper within the factory. Eli raised a hand, signaling them to stop.

Carrie leaned in close. "That's her, isn't it?"

"Could be," Eli whispered. "Let's move slow."

They edged closer, the voices growing louder. Eli motioned for Cole to take point. He slipped ahead, disappearing into the shadows. After a tense moment, he reappeared, signaling them forward.

Eli led them into an open room, and there, in the center, was a woman. She stood in front of an old desk, rifling through papers, a laptop open beside her. Her back was turned, but Eli could see the blonde hair Ramirez had described.

Before they could make a move, a gun cocked from the shadows. A tall figure emerged from behind a stack of crates, his weapon trained on Eli. Another figure stepped out from the opposite side, a woman with dark hair and cold eyes.

"Drop the guns," the tall man growled.

Carrie hesitated, her eyes flicking to Eli. He nodded slowly, and they lowered their weapons to the floor.

The blonde woman at the desk turned around, her eyes narrowing when she saw Eli. She was younger than he expected, mid-thirties, with sharp features and an air of authority.

"You've come a long way, Mr. Shepherd," she said, her voice calm. "But you're too late. The files aren't here."

Eli stepped forward, keeping his voice steady. "Then where are they?"

The woman smiled slightly. "Someplace safe. Grayson's files are too dangerous to fall into Lincoln's hands—or yours."

"Who are you?" Eli demanded, frustration boiling beneath the surface. "What do you know about my daughter?"

The woman's smile faded. "I'm sorry about Lily. But you don't understand what's really happening here. Grayson wasn't the only one playing this game. There are people much bigger than Lincoln, people who would burn this entire city to the ground to keep those files hidden."

Carrie's eyes widened. "Bigger than Lincoln? Who are you working for?"

The woman shook her head. "It doesn't matter. What matters is that you walk away now, while you still can. This is your only warning."

Eli stepped closer, his jaw clenched. "I'm not walking away. Not until I know what happened to Lily."

The woman stared at him for a long moment, her eyes searching his. Then, with a sigh, she nodded to the man with the gun. "Let them go."

Carrie looked at Eli, surprised. "Just like that?"

The woman's gaze hardened. "You've already lost too much, Mr. Shepherd. Don't lose more."

Eli didn't move. His heart pounded in his chest, every instinct telling him to push further, to fight. But something in the woman's eyes—a warning, a plea—held him back.

Finally, he nodded. "This isn't over."

The woman didn't respond. She turned back to the desk, her fingers tapping quickly on the laptop keys.

As they backed out of the room, Eli's mind raced. They were in deeper than they had ever imagined. And somewhere, buried beneath layers of conspiracy and blood, lay the truth about Lily.

As they left the factory, Cole glanced at Eli. "What now?"

Eli didn't answer right away. His eyes remained fixed on the building, his thoughts swirling with uncertainty and rage.

"We find out who's really pulling the strings," he finally said, his voice low. "And we burn them down."

# Chapter 8: Into the Serpent's Den

The hum of the engine filled the car as they sped through the dark, empty streets, heading for the only lead they had left: a name that Carrie had managed to pull from a stray comment the woman made back at the factory—**David Faraday**.

Faraday wasn't a name you found in the regular channels. He was buried deep in the intelligence world, a ghost even to people who made it their job to find ghosts. But Eli knew that name well. It had surfaced in a few classified ops during his time in military intelligence. Faraday had ties to shadow organizations, ones that didn't officially exist, yet influenced every major political decision from the shadows.

Carrie broke the silence. "Faraday's dangerous, Eli. If he's involved, this is bigger than we thought. Grayson was probably just one piece in a much larger puzzle."

Eli's grip tightened on the wheel. "Faraday's not just dangerous—he's untouchable. But if he's involved in this, he's tied to Lincoln somehow. He has to be."

Cole, who had remained quiet since the encounter at the factory, finally spoke. "Faraday runs black ops, does the kind of work governments won't admit to. If Grayson was mixed up with him, it's no wonder he had those files. Grayson probably thought the leverage could keep him alive."

"Obviously didn't work," Carrie said dryly. "We need a way in—if we just charge at Faraday, we'll be dead before we get two feet through the door."

Eli nodded, his mind racing. "We'll need someone who can give us access to Faraday's network. There's a guy I know—Peter Vaughn. Used to be CIA before he went private. He knows how to navigate Faraday's world."

Carrie raised an eyebrow. "More friends with shady pasts? You have a type."

Eli didn't respond to the joke. His mind was already focused on their next move. Vaughn owed him a favor, and if anyone could help them find Faraday, it was him.

**Vaughn's Safehouse – 3:30 AM**

Vaughn's "safehouse" was far from inconspicuous. Tucked into a posh neighborhood, it looked like any other luxurious home. But beneath the veneer of normalcy, Eli knew there was a fortress—Vaughn had designed it himself, complete with high-tech security and panic rooms hidden beneath the house.

Eli knocked on the door, and after a moment, a man with graying hair and sharp eyes appeared. Peter Vaughn had aged, but his intelligence was as razor-sharp as ever.

"Eli," Vaughn said, surprised. "You really know how to pick your hours."

"I need a favor," Eli replied without preamble, stepping inside.

Vaughn sighed, but there was a wry smile on his face. "You're lucky I owe you. What is it this time?"

Eli didn't waste time. "David Faraday. I need access to him."

The name wiped the smile from Vaughn's face. He gestured for them to sit and poured himself a drink. "Faraday? You have no idea what you're stepping into, Eli. The man doesn't just run in dangerous circles—he *is* the circle. He's protected by layers of deniability, with contacts in every government agency that matters. You go after him, you'll be on everyone's radar."

Carrie leaned forward. "We don't have a choice. He's involved in something big—bigger than Lincoln."

Vaughn studied them for a moment before nodding. "Alright. I'll get you in touch with someone who knows Faraday's current whereabouts. But if this goes sideways, I never knew you."

Eli gave him a grim smile. "Fair enough."

**The Meeting – 6:00 AM**

They met Vaughn's contact at a diner just outside the city. It was an old, rundown place where no one paid attention to who came and went. The man they were meeting—**Jericho**—was a former operative, now working in the grey market, dealing with information and covert operations.

Jericho was already seated when they arrived, his face partially hidden behind a newspaper. He didn't look up as they slid into the booth.

"You're looking for Faraday," he said, his voice low and gravely. "You must have a death wish."

"We need to know where he is," Eli said, cutting to the chase. "And how to get to him."

Jericho finally set the newspaper down, his eyes narrowing as he studied Eli. "Faraday doesn't meet with just anyone. He's untouchable, as you probably know. But he has one weakness—he holds quarterly meetings with a select group of international elites. People who trade secrets for influence. It's happening tomorrow night, at an estate just outside the city. That's your best chance."

Carrie frowned. "What kind of meeting?"

Jericho smiled thinly. "The kind where global deals are made, wars are started, and people disappear."

Eli felt a knot form in his stomach. It sounded like exactly the kind of place where Lily's fate might be sealed—where powerful people decided the lives of those beneath them without a second thought.

"Who's on the guest list?" Carrie asked, her voice tight.

Jericho shrugged. "Anyone with enough money or power to influence governments. Tech moguls, defense contractors, foreignsters. And Faraday runs the show, of course."

Eli exchanged a glance with Carrie. This was it. The door to Faraday's world. But it wasn't going to be easy to get in.

Jericho slid a piece of paper across the table. "You'll need this—Faraday's personal encryption key. It'll get you past the first layer of security. After that, you're on your own."

Eli pocketed the paper, nodding. "Thanks."

Jericho smirked. "Don't thank me yet. You're walking into the lion's den. If you make it out alive, then you can thank me."

**The Estate – The Next Night**

The estate loomed ahead, a sprawling mansion surrounded by thick, well-manicured forests. It was the kind of place where secrets were buried, where the rich and powerful could do anything without consequence.

Eli, Carrie, and Cole pulled up to the gates in a black SUV they had borrowed—well, stolen—for the occasion. The security was tight, with armed guards patrolling the perimeter. But with Jericho's encryption key, they were able to slip past the first checkpoint without raising alarms.

The mansion itself was buzzing with activity—luxury cars pulled up to the entrance, well-dressed men and women stepping out and being escorted inside by security.

"We blend in," Eli said quietly. "We find Faraday, and we get answers. But keep your eyes open—there's no telling who else is here."

They entered the grand foyer, their eyes scanning the room filled with political powerhouses and shadowy figures. Eli's gut tightened. He had spent years in this world, dealing with people like this—people who saw the world as a chessboard, with human lives as expendable pawns.

But this time, it was personal.

Carrie leaned in close. "Do you see him?"

Eli shook his head, but his eyes never stopped moving. Faraday was here somewhere, pulling the strings. And if Grayson's files were still in play, it was likely the entire city was about to become a battlefield for control over them.

They slipped through the crowd, moving deeper into the mansion. Eli's heart pounded in his chest. They were on enemy turf now, surrounded by people who wouldn't hesitate to kill them if they got in the way.

And then he saw him.

David Faraday stood near the back of the room, speaking with a group of men in expensive suits. He was exactly as Eli remembered—tall, with a commanding presence and a calculating gaze. This was the man who held the answers. The man who could lead Eli to the truth about Lily.

Eli's fists clenched. The time for waiting was over.

"Carrie," he said, his voice cold. "We're going in."

**The chilling Realization**

The next few moments were a blur. Eli pushed through the crowd, his eyes locked on Faraday. Every muscle in his body was tense, ready to strike. But as they closed in, something went wrong.

Faraday glanced up, his eyes meeting Eli's.

And he smiled.

Before Eli could react, the lights in the mansion flickered. The security systems activated, and guards flooded the room.

They had been made.

Eli cursed under his breath as he and Carrie drew their weapons, the crowd erupting into chaos around them.

But Faraday didn't run. He stood calmly, as if he had expected them all along.

As the guards closed in, Eli realized something chilling: Faraday had been waiting for this. They weren't the hunters.

They were the prey.

# Chapter 9: The Snare Tightens

Chaos erupted in the mansion as guests screamed and scrambled for the exits. Eli felt the adrenaline surge through him, sharpening his focus. He had to get to Faraday, had to find out what he knew about Lily and the files.

"Stay close!" Eli shouted to Carrie and Cole, but the noise of gunfire echoed, drowning out his voice. He pushed through the throng, aiming for Faraday, who remained eerily calm amidst the pandemonium.

"Do you really think you can take me down, Eli?" Faraday called out, his voice smooth and mocking. "You've walked right into my trap."

Eli's heart raced. The man was unhinged, a puppet master who reveled in his control. Eli had no time for games. He surged forward, dodging the scattering crowd and the guards who were trying to restore order.

"Faraday!" he yelled, but the man simply smiled, his eyes glinting with malice.

In the corner of the room, Carrie and Cole were working to create a path through the chaos. Carrie's gun was raised, firing off warning shots that sent a few guards ducking for cover. "Eli, we need to flank him!" she shouted, her voice steady despite the turmoil.

Eli nodded, cutting left toward the bar, where the chaos was thickest. "We need to get out of this crowd!"

As he moved, he felt a presence behind him. A guard lunged, tackling him to the ground. Eli struggled, throwing punches as the guard pinned him down. Just as he was about to overpower him, Cole appeared, grabbing the guard by the collar and yanking him away.

"Get up!" Cole shouted, pulling Eli to his feet. "We have to move!"

Eli scanned the room again, spotting Faraday slipping away through a side door, flanked by two armed men. "There!" he pointed, but Carrie had already spotted the same exit.

"Go!" she yelled, leading the charge. They sprinted toward the door, but just as they reached it, a surge of guards blocked their path, weapons drawn.

"Drop your weapons!" one of them commanded, his voice firm and authoritative.

Eli hesitated. They were surrounded. He could feel the weight of the moment, the realization that they were in over their heads. But he couldn't back down now—not when they were so close to the answers they desperately needed.

"We're not going to let you take us in!" Eli shouted, raising his gun.

"Eli, wait!" Carrie shouted, but it was too late.

A gunfight erupted in the hallway. Eli fired at the guards, trying to create a path. Bullets flew, the air thick with smoke and adrenaline. He caught sight of Faraday slipping through a door at the end of the corridor, his laughter echoing like a taunt.

"Get him!" Eli yelled, but they were outnumbered. The guards advanced, and Eli felt the pressure closing in.

"Fall back!" Carrie shouted, pulling Eli away as another barrage of bullets tore through the air, narrowly missing them.

They turned, retreating deeper into the mansion, searching for an exit, but the guards were relentless. The chaos of the party outside was now a distant memory, the laughter replaced by the sounds of violence.

"Where do we go?" Cole panted, scanning the hallways for an escape.

"Up!" Eli shouted, pointing to a staircase leading to the upper floors. "We can regroup there!"

They sprinted up the stairs, but Eli could hear the guards following. Time was running out. They burst into a large room, filled with expensive furniture and a sweeping view of the estate's grounds.

"Barricade the door!" Carrie shouted, and they quickly pushed a heavy desk against it.

"Do you think it will hold?" Cole asked, breathless.

"It'll buy us time," Eli said, glancing around the room. He spotted a window that overlooked the garden below. "We can climb out there."

Carrie nodded, glancing back at the door. "How much time do we have?"

"Not long." Eli moved to the window, trying to pry it open. It was stuck. "Help me!"

As they struggled with the window, they heard voices approaching from the stairwell. The guards were almost upon them.

"Eli!" Carrie called, panic creeping into her voice. "We need to move!"

With a final shove, the window creaked open. Eli climbed through first, dropping into the garden below, landing on soft grass. He looked up just in time to see Carrie and Cole follow.

"Go!" Eli urged, glancing back at the mansion. The guards would be out any second.

They sprinted across the garden, ducking behind hedges and statues, hearts racing as they made their way to the edge of the property. Just as they reached the outer wall, gunfire erupted behind them.

"Keep moving!" Eli shouted, adrenaline pushing them forward.

They ducked and weaved through the darkness, heading for a thicket of trees that lined the estate's perimeter. The sound of shouts and footsteps behind them urged them on.

Finally, they reached the treeline, and Eli halted, catching his breath. "We need to get off the property. We can't stay here."

Carrie looked back at the mansion, fear etched on her face. "What about Faraday? He's still in there!"

Eli hesitated, weighing their options. "We can't save him tonight. We need to regroup and come up with a new plan."

Cole nodded, glancing around. "There's a road a bit further back. If we can get to it, we might find a way to call for backup."

"Let's move!" Eli urged, leading the way into the trees.

They navigated through the underbrush, adrenaline still coursing through their veins. The sound of gunfire faded, but the threat lingered, a shadow over their escape.

As they neared the road, Eli's mind was racing. They had come so close to Faraday, yet now they were running for their lives. But he knew they would have another chance. They had to.

Finally, they broke through the trees, emerging onto a secluded road illuminated by the soft glow of streetlights. Eli scanned the area, spotting a small pull-off where they could hide for a moment.

"Let's catch our breath," he said, leading them to the edge of the road.

Carrie leaned against a tree, breathing heavily. "What now? We've lost our shot at Faraday, and Lincoln is still out there."

Eli looked at them, determination hardening his features. "We regroup, we plan, and we go back for Faraday. He has the answers we need."

"But how?" Cole asked, frustration evident. "He's going to be on high alert now."

Eli paused, considering their options. "We need to think bigger. We need allies—people who can help us get close to Faraday again. If we can turn the tides, we might be able to force his hand."

Carrie nodded slowly, her resolve returning. "We can reach out to some contacts of my own. People who know how to operate in the shadows."

Eli's heart lifted slightly. "Good. We'll find a way to get to him, and this time, we won't be walking into a trap."

As they huddled together, plotting their next move, Eli felt the weight of the world pressing down on him. The clock was ticking, and with each passing hour, Lily's fate hung in the balance.

But one thing was clear—he wasn't going to give up. Not now. Not ever. They would uncover the truth, and they would bring everyone responsible to justice.

Even if it meant wading through the darkest depths of a conspiracy that threatened to consume them all.

# Chapter 10: Shadows and Alliances

The sun began to rise, casting a pale light over the trees as Eli, Carrie, and Cole settled into a hidden spot off the roadside. They couldn't linger too long; the guards would be searching for them, and the longer they stayed exposed, the greater the risk.

"Let's figure out our next move," Eli said, his voice steady but low. "We need to find a way to reach out to my contacts and Carrie's."

Carrie nodded, her expression resolute. "I can get in touch with a few people from my past in law enforcement. They might have insights into Lincoln's operations and even connections to Faraday."

Cole rubbed the back of his neck, still on edge. "I can reach out to a buddy from my time in the service. He's got ties in the private security sector. If we can get some intel on Faraday's movements, it might help us get closer."

"Good," Eli replied, a plan forming in his mind. "We'll split up. Carrie and I will take the lead on reaching out to contacts, while Cole makes his call. We'll meet back here in two hours."

"Sounds good," Carrie said. "But let's be careful. We can't afford any slip-ups."

They exchanged quick nods before heading their separate ways, each carrying the weight of their mission.

### The Local Diner – 9:30 AM

Eli and Carrie entered a small diner, the kind that had seen better days but still served a mean cup of coffee. It was the perfect place to lay low and make calls without drawing attention.

"Let's grab a booth in the back," Eli suggested, scanning the room for any potential threats. Once seated, he pulled out his phone and began scrolling through his contacts, looking for someone who could help.

Carrie took a sip of her coffee, her expression thoughtful. "You think your contacts will take you seriously after all this time?"

Eli shrugged, tapping the screen. "They'll listen. I know how to appeal to their sense of duty. If I frame it right, they'll want to help."

Just as he was about to dial, his phone buzzed with a message. It was from an old colleague, **Mark Jefferson**—a former analyst with the agency who had deep connections within the intelligence community.

**Mark Jefferson: Heard you're back in town. We need to talk. Urgent.**

Eli looked at Carrie, a mixture of hope and anxiety in his eyes. "It's Mark. He wants to meet."

"Good sign?" she asked.

"Could be," Eli replied, heart racing. "He might have insights into Faraday or Lincoln. But it could also mean trouble."

"Then we should go," Carrie urged. "If we can get even a hint of what we're dealing with, it'll make our next move easier."

"Alright," Eli said, texting back a quick response to meet at a nearby park. "Let's see what he knows."

### The Park – 10:30 AM

They arrived at the park, a quiet place filled with trees and winding paths. Eli spotted Mark sitting on a bench, his eyes scanning the surroundings. He looked older than Eli remembered—grayer and more worn—but his presence still radiated authority.

Eli approached, a nod of acknowledgment exchanged. "Mark."

"Eli," Mark replied, his voice low. "I didn't think you'd come back here after everything."

"I didn't have a choice," Eli said, taking a seat beside him. "I need your help. Things are bad—Lincoln's involved, and we're trying to track down David Faraday."

Mark's expression darkened. "You're playing a dangerous game. Faraday is not someone to take lightly."

"I know. But I need to know what he's up to and how he's tied to Lincoln. Lives are on the line, including my daughter's," Eli said, urgency creeping into his voice.

Mark studied Eli for a moment, weighing his options. "Alright. I can give you some intel. But you need to be cautious. The walls have ears, and you can't trust anyone in this game."

Carrie leaned in, her eyes intense. "What do you know?"

"Faraday has been working on a deal involving data extraction—files from multiple agencies, including sensitive personal information that could topple governments," Mark explained. "Lincoln is likely trying to secure that information for himself. If he gets it, the fallout will be catastrophic."

Eli felt his stomach knot. "And the files Grayson had? Are they part of this?"

"Yes," Mark confirmed. "They're pivotal to what Faraday is orchestrating. Grayson's files could expose not just Lincoln but the entire operation. If you want to find your daughter, you need to get those files first."

Carrie glanced at Eli, her mind racing. "How do we get to them?"

"Faraday has a secure location—an offshore facility where he's been keeping the data," Mark said, lowering his voice further. "He rotates his security frequently, but I can get you access codes for a limited window. You'll have to act fast."

Eli leaned forward, gripping the edge of the bench. "When?"

"Tonight. But you need to be prepared for heavy security. This isn't a simple infiltration. You'll be going against some of the best."

Eli's mind raced with the implications. "We'll do whatever it takes."

"Just remember," Mark warned, his eyes serious. "If you get caught, there's no coming back from it. Faraday won't just lock you up—he'll make sure you disappear."

Carrie's expression was steely. "We won't get caught. We're ready for this."

"Good," Mark said, standing up. "I'll send you the codes. But be careful, Eli. You're stepping into the lion's den. The stakes are higher than you realize."

As Mark walked away, Eli felt a mix of fear and determination. They had a shot now, a chance to uncover the truth. But the clock was ticking, and with every moment they waited, Lily's fate hung in the balance.

**The Abandoned Warehouse – Evening**

Back at their temporary hideout, Eli, Carrie, and Cole gathered to go over their plan. The atmosphere was tense but focused.

"Mark's intel says we have a two-hour window," Eli said, spreading out a map of the facility on the table. "We'll approach from the east side, where the surveillance is weakest. We'll split up to create a distraction while one of us goes for the files."

Carrie nodded. "I'll take point on the extraction. I've got the best chance of getting in without raising alarms."

Cole leaned back in his chair, his brow furrowed. "What if things go south? We need an exit strategy."

Eli considered this. "If we're compromised, we regroup at the secondary rendezvous point near the docks. We need to stay flexible."

The room fell silent as they each mentally prepared for the mission ahead. Eli could feel the weight of their lives resting on this one night. This was their chance to uncover the truth, to find Lily, and to dismantle the forces threatening everything they held dear.

As the hour approached, they gathered their gear, each of them steeling themselves for the fight to come. Eli's heart raced with a mixture of fear and hope. This was it—their moment to confront the darkness that had haunted them for so long.

"Let's do this," Eli said, his voice steady. "For Lily."

"For Lily," Carrie and Cole echoed, their resolve unyielding.

And with that, they stepped into the night, ready to face whatever shadows awaited them in the depths of Faraday's lair.

# Chapter 11: Breaching the Fortress

The night was cloaked in darkness as Eli, Carrie, and Cole made their way to the abandoned warehouse on the outskirts of town. It loomed ahead like a ghost from the past—its windows darkened, its walls weathered. A perfect front for what lay beneath: a fortress of secrets and lies.

Eli checked his watch. "We have to move quickly. The window Mark gave us won't last long."

Carrie nodded, her expression focused. "I'll take the lead. Keep your eyes open for guards."

They approached the east side of the warehouse, where shadows danced under the pale moonlight. Eli could feel his pulse quicken; this was the moment they had been preparing for.

"Okay, let's go," Eli whispered, leading them to a side door that was slightly ajar.

Carrie slipped inside first, her movements graceful and deliberate. Eli followed, with Cole bringing up the rear. The inside was dimly lit, the air thick with the smell of oil and rust. They quickly scanned the area—stacks of crates, old machinery, and the distant hum of generators filled the space.

Eli pointed to a narrow corridor leading deeper into the warehouse. "That's our route. The files should be in the secured data room on the other side."

Carrie gestured for them to follow, her instincts kicking in. They crept along the corridor, eyes peeled for any sign of security. The low buzz of machinery masked their footsteps, allowing them to move undetected.

**The Data Room – 10:30 PM**

They reached a large door labeled **DATA ROOM**. Eli pressed his ear against it, listening for any sounds inside. Silence. He glanced at Carrie, who nodded, signaling readiness.

"On three," Eli whispered. "One... two... three!"

They burst through the door, guns drawn, but the room was empty except for a series of computer terminals and locked cabinets. The sight both relieved and frustrated Eli. "No guards. We might actually pull this off."

Carrie rushed to a terminal, quickly typing in the access codes Mark had provided. The screen blinked to life, displaying a series of files and folders. "I'm in! Let's find those files."

As Carrie scrolled through the data, Eli moved to the locked cabinets, searching for the ones that might contain physical copies of the files. Cole stood guard near the door, scanning the corridor for any signs of trouble.

"Here!" Carrie exclaimed, her voice low with urgency. "I found the files—everything we need! But it's all digital. We'll need to download it to a drive."

"Do we have time?" Eli asked, glancing toward the door.

"I'll make it quick," she replied, plugging in a USB drive.

Suddenly, a loud alarm blared, piercing through the warehouse. Red lights flashed, illuminating the room in an ominous glow.

"Damn it!" Eli cursed, rushing to the door. "We've been compromised! Cole, get ready!"

Carrie's fingers flew over the keyboard, her focus unwavering. "Almost done! Just a few more seconds!"

The sound of boots echoed down the corridor. Eli's heart raced. "We don't have time! We need to move now!"

"Done!" Carrie shouted, yanking the drive from the terminal just as the door began to rattle.

Eli pushed her behind him, readying his weapon. "Get ready to run!"

The door burst open, and two guards stormed in, guns raised. Eli fired without hesitation, hitting one guard in the shoulder. The other ducked, returning fire.

"Go!" Eli shouted, his voice booming over the chaos.

Carrie bolted past him, sprinting down the corridor. Cole followed, covering their retreat as Eli fired another shot, hitting the second guard in the leg.

They dashed into the darkness, moving quickly but cautiously through the maze of the warehouse. The alarm continued to wail, adding to the sense of urgency.

"Which way?" Cole yelled, glancing back at the pursuing guards.

Eli pointed down another corridor. "That way! We'll find an exit!"

**The Main Floor – 10:40 PM**

They sprinted toward the main floor, adrenaline pushing them forward. The sound of footsteps echoed behind them, growing louder with each passing second.

Eli led the way, his heart pounding in rhythm with his footsteps. As they reached the open space, they spotted a large garage door at the far end. It was their best chance for escape.

"Keep moving!" Eli urged, but just as they neared the door, it began to close.

"No!" Carrie cried, rushing forward.

"Wait!" Eli yelled, grabbing her arm. "There's no time!"

Cole raised his gun, prepared to shoot at the mechanism, but Eli shook his head. "No! We'll be trapped. We need another way!"

The guards were closing in, their shouts echoing through the warehouse.

"Back!" Eli ordered, retreating into the shadows as they tried to find cover.

As they ducked behind a stack of crates, Eli's mind raced. They couldn't get pinned down here. There had to be another exit.

"Over there!" Carrie pointed to a set of double doors at the far side, slightly ajar. "That might lead to the loading dock!"

Eli nodded, ready to move. "On three. One... two... three!"

They burst from their hiding place, sprinting toward the double doors. Bullets ricocheted off the metal shelves around them, but they pushed through, adrenaline propelling them forward.

**The Loading Dock – 10:45 PM**

They pushed through the double doors and skidded to a stop. The loading dock was dimly lit, filled with crates and old machinery. A large truck was parked in the center, its back door open.

"Get in!" Eli yelled, rushing toward the truck.

Carrie and Cole scrambled into the back, and Eli climbed in behind them, quickly shutting the door. They could hear the guards shouting outside, closing in on their position.

"Start it!" Eli commanded Cole, who was already rifling through the driver's compartment.

"Got it!" Cole replied, turning the ignition. The truck roared to life, and they felt a surge of hope.

"Let's move!" Eli shouted.

As they pulled away from the loading dock, the sound of gunfire rang out, bullets hitting the metal walls. The truck jolted as Cole hit the gas, careening out of the warehouse and onto the road.

"Hold on!" Cole yelled, steering wildly to avoid the barricades.

Eli turned back to see shadows rushing from the warehouse, but they were already gaining distance. The thrill of escape coursed through him.

**On the Road – 10:50 PM**

As they sped down the empty road, the adrenaline began to fade, replaced by the weight of what they had just done. Carrie leaned against the back wall, catching her breath.

"I can't believe we actually made it out," she said, disbelief lacing her tone.

Eli let out a breath he didn't realize he was holding. "We still have a lot to do. We need to review the files and figure out our next move."

Cole glanced back at them, his face tense. "Did we get everything? Are we sure?"

Carrie pulled out the USB drive, holding it up triumphantly. "We got it! All the data we need."

Eli felt a surge of determination. "Then let's get to a safe place. We need to analyze everything and find a way to use it against Faraday and Lincoln."

They drove in silence for a moment, the reality of their situation settling in. The mission was far from over, and the stakes had never been higher.

"Where to?" Cole asked, breaking the silence.

Eli thought for a moment. "There's an old safehouse I used to use. It's off the grid—no one will find us there. We can regroup and figure out our next steps."

"Sounds good," Carrie said, her voice steady.

As they continued down the road, Eli felt the adrenaline of the night begin to wear off. But a new sense of purpose ignited within him. They had the files. They had a chance to expose the truth.

And he was willing to do whatever it took to protect his family and dismantle the web of corruption that threatened to consume them all.

# Chapter 12: The Calm Before the Storm

The old safehouse was a relic of Eli's past, nestled in a secluded area surrounded by dense woods. It was unassuming, a small cabin with peeling paint and a rusted roof, but it provided the privacy they desperately needed.

As they pulled up, Eli scanned the surroundings, ensuring no one had followed them. "We're clear," he said, stepping out of the truck. "Let's get inside."

Carrie and Cole followed him inside, the musty air filling their lungs as they entered. The interior was bare, with a few mismatched pieces of furniture and a small kitchenette. Eli flicked on a light, illuminating the space.

"We should set up here," he said, moving to a dusty table in the corner. "Let's take a look at those files."

Carrie connected the USB drive to a laptop that had seen better days, her fingers moving swiftly as she navigated through the data. "This might take a bit to sort through," she said, her eyes focused on the screen.

Eli paced the small space, the weight of the night's events pressing down on him. He couldn't shake the feeling of dread that had settled in his stomach. "We need to stay alert. Faraday won't take kindly to us getting away with his data."

Cole nodded, leaning against the wall. "He'll come after us. We need a plan."

"Once we know what we're dealing with," Eli said, glancing at Carrie, "we can figure out our next move."

As the minutes passed, Carrie's expression shifted from concentration to shock. "Eli, you need to see this."

Eli rushed over, peering at the screen. "What is it?"

Carrie pointed to a folder labeled **OPERATION NIGHTFALL**. "This contains everything—data files, surveillance photos, even communication logs between Faraday and Lincoln. It's like a roadmap of their entire operation."

"Show me," Eli said, heart racing as he scanned through the documents.

The files revealed a shocking web of connections: corrupt officials, money laundering schemes, and a timeline of events leading up to the potential data leak that could upend national security. Eli felt the weight of the implications crashing down on him.

"This is huge," he breathed, adrenaline surging. "If we expose this—"

"Eli, look at this," Carrie interrupted, pointing to a specific entry. "This is dated just a few days ago. It mentions a meeting between Faraday and Lincoln at a location we recognize."

"Where?" Cole asked, moving closer.

"A private yacht," Carrie replied, her eyes wide. "It's docked at the marina just outside of town. They're planning something big."

Eli felt a mix of excitement and fear. "We need to crash that meeting."

"But how?" Cole asked, raising an eyebrow. "We don't have backup. It'll be crawling with guards."

Eli thought for a moment. "We use the data. We leak this information to the press and expose them publicly. If we can create enough chaos, we might force them to reveal themselves."

Carrie shook her head. "That's risky. If they catch wind of us, they'll eliminate the threat before it even gets out."

"Then we need to be smarter about it," Eli said, determination hardening his voice. "We need a distraction. If we can create a situation that draws attention away from the yacht, we can get in undetected."

Cole crossed his arms, considering. "What about the marina's security? They probably have cameras everywhere."

Carrie's eyes lit up. "I could hack into the security system remotely. If I can disable the cameras for a short window, we might have a shot."

Eli felt hope stirring. "That could work. But we'll need to time it perfectly."

They gathered around the laptop, diving deeper into the files. Carrie identified the security protocols for the marina, while Eli and Cole plotted their approach.

"Once we're in, we'll split up," Eli instructed. "I'll go for Faraday and Lincoln. Carrie, you gather evidence—anything that can be used to expose them. Cole, you keep watch and cover our escape."

As they outlined their plan, the sense of urgency intensified. They had to act quickly; time was running out, and the danger was ever-present.

**The Planning Session**

Hours flew by as they honed their strategy. Eli felt the tension in the air, the weight of the stakes pushing them all to their limits. Finally, Carrie closed the laptop, a determined look on her face. "I'm ready. If we're going to do this, we need to move now."

Eli nodded, adrenaline coursing through him. "Let's gear up and hit the road."

They quickly gathered their things, loading up on supplies and weapons before slipping back into the night. The truck's engine rumbled to life, and they drove toward the marina, the moonlight casting an eerie glow on the winding road.

### The Marina – Midnight

As they approached the marina, Eli's heart raced. The night was quiet, but the tension was palpable. The sound of waves lapping against the dock provided an unsettling backdrop to their mission.

"Alright," Eli said, pulling into a shadowy spot near the entrance. "Let's stick to the plan. Carrie, you're on the cameras. Cole, stay alert. I'll take point."

Carrie nodded, pulling out her laptop. "I'll need a few minutes to access the system. I'll let you know when I'm in."

Eli and Cole stepped out, scanning the area. A few guards were patrolling, their flashlights cutting through the darkness. Eli could feel the adrenaline spike again.

"Stay low and keep your voices down," Eli whispered as they crept toward the main dock.

Carrie's fingers flew over the keyboard, her focus intense. "Almost there... just a few more seconds."

As Eli and Cole inched closer to the dock, they spotted the yacht—a luxurious vessel lit with soft lights, a stark contrast to the shadows around them.

"We need to wait for the guards to pass," Eli said, glancing back at Carrie. "How much longer?"

"Just about there!" Carrie replied, her voice tense. "And... got it! Cameras are disabled for the next five minutes!"

Eli nodded. "Now's our chance!"

They dashed toward the yacht, moving quickly but quietly. Eli's heart raced as they approached the side of the vessel, scanning for a way to board.

"Over here!" Cole pointed to a small boarding ladder.

Eli climbed first, followed closely by Cole. Once aboard, they quickly surveyed the deck. It was eerily quiet, the only sounds coming from the gentle rocking of the yacht.

"Stay sharp," Eli whispered, moving stealthily across the deck.

They descended into the main cabin, where they found a luxurious interior, complete with plush seating and expensive art lining the walls.

"Let's split up," Eli said, his voice barely above a whisper. "I'll check the main office. You two search the living quarters."

Cole nodded, glancing around. "Let's meet back here in five minutes."

Eli moved toward the office, heart pounding. He pushed open the door, his instincts on high alert. The office was filled with papers, documents, and a laptop left open on the desk.

"Come on, come on," he muttered, scanning the papers for anything relevant.

Just then, a voice echoed from the upper deck. "You sure this is a good idea, Lincoln? We're taking a big risk here."

Eli froze, recognizing the voice immediately. It was Faraday. He was here, and Lincoln was with him.

"Trust me, David," Lincoln's voice replied, smooth and calculated. "The payoff will be worth it."

Eli's heart raced as he crouched down, hidden from view. He needed to hear more.

"They'll never suspect a thing," Lincoln continued. "By the time they realize what's happening, we'll be long gone, with the data in our hands."

Eli's blood ran cold. They were planning to leave, likely with the sensitive data that could bring them down.

"Do you think Eli is still out there?" Faraday asked, a hint of worry in his tone.

Eli's breath caught in his throat. They were onto him.

"Let him come. He's a fool if he thinks he can stop us now," Lincoln replied dismissively. "We have everything we need."

Eli clenched his fists, anger boiling within him. They couldn't escape. Not this time.

As the two men continued their conversation, Eli pulled out his phone, discreetly recording their voices. He had to gather evidence. He would expose them, no matter the risk.

Suddenly, a loud crash echoed from the living quarters. Cole's voice shouted, "Get away from her!"

Eli's heart dropped. He bolted from the office, racing toward the noise. As he reached the living room, he saw Carrie grappling with one of the guards, her determination shining through.

"Eli!" she shouted, struggling against the guard's grip.

"Get down!" Eli yelled, rushing forward.

In a split second, Eli drew his weapon, firing at the guard. The shot hit its mark, and the guard crumpled to the floor, freeing Carrie from his grasp.

"Are you alright?" Eli asked, his breath quickening.

"I'm fine! But we need to move!" Carrie replied, adrenaline pumping through her veins.

Suddenly, Lincoln and Faraday appeared at the top of the stairs, eyes wide with shock. "What the hell is going on?" Lincoln shouted.

"Run!" Eli yelled, grabbing Carrie's hand.

# Chapter 13: The Reckoning

Eli and Carrie dashed toward the back of the yacht, adrenaline surging as they heard Lincoln's voice barking orders. The sound of hurried footsteps echoed behind them—Faraday and Lincoln were coming for them.

"Where's Cole?" Carrie panted, glancing over her shoulder.

"Covering our exit, I hope!" Eli replied, his mind racing. They needed to find a way off this yacht and fast.

They reached a door leading to the lower deck, where the noise of the ocean was muffled. Eli flung it open, revealing a narrow hallway lined with doors.

"Let's check here!" Eli said, pulling Carrie inside one of the cabins. He shut the door, pressing his ear against it to listen.

"Do you think they saw us?" Carrie whispered, her breath coming in quick bursts.

"I don't know," Eli replied, his heart pounding. "But we can't stay here."

They could hear voices approaching, the sound of footsteps getting louder. Eli turned, scanning the small cabin for anything they could use. A heavy fire extinguisher hung on the wall, and he grabbed it, feeling the weight of it in his hands.

"Stay close," he said. "We'll have to be ready to fight our way out."

Just then, the door rattled as someone tried to open it. "They're coming!" Carrie exclaimed.

Eli braced himself, ready to use the extinguisher as a weapon. The door swung open, and Lincoln stepped inside, followed closely by Faraday.

"Got you!" Lincoln sneered, his eyes gleaming with arrogance. "Did you really think you could escape?"

Eli swung the extinguisher, catching Lincoln off guard and knocking him to the ground. The sudden chaos erupted into action as Faraday lunged forward, grabbing Carrie.

"Get off her!" Eli shouted, rushing to help her.

Cole burst into the cabin just in time, tackling Faraday and sending both of them crashing to the floor.

"Eli, I thought I lost you!" Cole shouted, struggling to restrain Faraday.

Eli rushed to Carrie's side, his heart pounding as he saw her grappling with Lincoln, who was scrambling to get back up.

"Get the laptop!" Carrie yelled, her voice filled with urgency. "We need the evidence!"

Eli glanced toward the desk, where the laptop still hummed with life. "I'll get it!" He dashed to grab it, feeling the heat of the confrontation behind him.

"Stop him!" Lincoln shouted, finally breaking free from Carrie's grasp.

Eli seized the laptop, but Lincoln lunged at him, catching Eli by the shoulder. Eli twisted around, shoving the laptop into Carrie's hands. "Go! Get it to safety!"

"Eli!" Carrie shouted, her eyes wide with fear.

"Just go!" Eli insisted, adrenaline coursing through him. He pushed Lincoln back, but the man was relentless, charging at him again.

Cole and Faraday were locked in a fierce struggle on the floor, each grappling for control. Eli needed to help them, but Lincoln was on him, forcing him to backpedal.

"Do you really think you can outsmart us?" Lincoln spat, his eyes narrowing with malice. "You're out of your depth, Eli!"

"Maybe," Eli shot back, quickly scanning the room for an advantage. He saw the fire extinguisher still in his hand. "But I'm not going down without a fight!"

With a swift movement, he swung the extinguisher again, catching Lincoln off balance. The man stumbled back, allowing Eli to dart past him toward Cole and Faraday.

"Get up!" Eli shouted as he joined Cole, helping him wrestle Faraday into a headlock.

"Let's finish this," Cole grunted, his muscles straining against Faraday's resistance.

Just as they were about to gain the upper hand, the yacht lurched violently, knocking them all off balance. The sudden motion threw Eli against the wall, and he struggled to regain his footing.

"What was that?" Carrie yelled from the doorway, clutching the laptop tightly.

"Don't know, but we need to move!" Eli shouted back, catching his breath.

Lincoln took advantage of the chaos, lunging at Carrie, but Eli shouted, "No!"

With a burst of energy, Eli rushed forward, tackling Lincoln to the ground before he could reach her. They crashed against a stack of crates, and Eli fought to pin Lincoln down.

"Cole, help me!" Eli grunted, struggling against Lincoln's weight.

Cole, still grappling with Faraday, finally managed to break free. He lunged forward, grabbing Lincoln by the arms and pulling him off Eli. Together, they forced him down, securing his hands behind his back with a length of rope that had been coiled on the deck.

"Now, Faraday!" Eli shouted, turning to face him.

But Faraday was already scrambling to his feet, eyes wild with rage. He charged at Eli, but Carrie swung the laptop bag like a weapon, catching him off guard.

"Get away from him!" she yelled, and the impact sent Faraday crashing against the wall.

Eli seized the moment, lunging at Faraday and pushing him down again. "You think you can run this operation without consequences? You've messed with the wrong people!"

The yacht lurched again, this time more violently. The alarms blared, and the lights flickered ominously.

"Something's wrong with the yacht!" Cole shouted, eyes wide. "We need to get off—now!"

"Where's the exit?" Carrie yelled, glancing around.

Eli took a deep breath, forcing clarity through the chaos. "The front deck! We can escape from there!"

With urgency, they rushed back toward the upper deck. The alarms echoed around them, adding to the chaos as they burst through the door.

**On the Deck – Midnight**

The scene was frantic. Crew members were scrambling to stabilize the yacht, and a few guards were attempting to restore order.

Eli glanced at the chaos around them. "We need to blend in and get to the edge of the dock!"

They moved swiftly, trying to stay out of sight. As they approached the edge, Eli spotted a small speedboat tied to the dock—a chance for escape.

"There!" he pointed, adrenaline surging again. "We can take that!"

They made their way toward the speedboat, but a guard spotted them and shouted, "Hey! Stop right there!"

"Go!" Eli yelled, adrenaline pumping through his veins.

Carrie sprinted ahead, leaping into the speedboat. "Get in!"

Eli and Cole followed, and as they jumped into the boat, Eli quickly untied it. "Start it up!" he commanded.

Carrie fumbled with the ignition, her fingers shaking. "Come on, come on!"

Eli looked back, seeing Lincoln and Faraday pushing through the crowd, determination etched on their faces. "We're out of time!"

"Got it!" Carrie exclaimed, and the engine roared to life.

"Let's go!" Eli shouted as they shot away from the dock, the water spraying behind them.

They sped away from the yacht, the chaos fading behind them. Eli felt a rush of relief wash over him, but it was short-lived. The mission was far from over.

"We need to get somewhere safe," he said, his voice filled with urgency. "Faraday and Lincoln won't stop coming for us."

Cole nodded, glancing back at the yacht, which was now just a silhouette against the moonlit water. "What's the plan?"

Eli took a deep breath, a new determination fueling him. "We take the fight to them. We expose everything we have, make sure the world knows what they're planning. But first, we need to regroup and strategize."

Carrie looked at him, her eyes fierce. "I'm with you. We're not backing down."

As the speedboat cut through the water, Eli felt the weight of their situation pressing down. They had uncovered a dangerous plot, but now the real battle was just beginning. They needed to stay one step ahead of their enemies, or risk losing everything.

"Hold on tight," Eli said, gripping the steering wheel as they headed into the darkness, ready to confront whatever awaited them.

# Chapter 14: The Storm Before the Dawn

As the speedboat sliced through the waves, Eli focused on the horizon, the dark outline of the coastline growing nearer. They needed a place to regroup and plan their next move, but time was against them. Faraday and Lincoln would be relentless.

"Where are we headed?" Cole asked, glancing back at the fading lights of the yacht.

Eli thought quickly. "There's a small fishing village a few miles up the coast. We can find somewhere to lay low and go over the files."

Carrie nodded, her fingers gripping the edge of the boat as the wind whipped around them. "We should be careful. They'll be looking for us, and we can't risk getting caught."

"Agreed," Eli replied, steering with determination. "We'll keep a low profile until we're ready to strike back."

As they approached the village, the dim lights of small houses flickered in the distance, casting a warm glow against the night. Eli maneuvered the boat toward a secluded cove, where they could dock without drawing attention.

Once they were secured, the trio quickly hopped out, keeping a watchful eye on their surroundings. Eli led the way up a narrow path that wound through the trees, leading to a rustic inn tucked away from prying eyes.

## THE INN – 1:00 AM

Inside the inn, the air was warm and inviting, a stark contrast to the chaos they had just escaped. The wooden beams creaked underfoot as they made their way to a small table in the corner, far from the gaze of any curious patrons.

Eli pulled out the laptop, opening it to the files they had downloaded. "Let's get to work. We need to analyze everything we've got."

Carrie leaned in, her expression serious. "We have to figure out how to expose Lincoln and Faraday without putting ourselves in too much danger."

Eli nodded, scrolling through the documents. "Here's the timeline. They've been planning this operation for months. If we can find a way to connect the dots, we can blow the whole thing wide open."

Cole furrowed his brow, looking at the screen. "What about the guards? They'll be expecting us to make a move soon."

"We can't act recklessly," Carrie cautioned. "We need solid evidence and a clear strategy. If we move too quickly, we risk losing everything."

Eli felt the weight of the decision pressing down on him. "What if we leak this information to a trusted journalist? Someone who can get it out to the public?"

Carrie considered this, nodding slowly. "That could work. But we need to be careful about who we trust. Faraday has eyes everywhere."

"Let's identify potential contacts," Cole suggested, leaning closer to the screen. "We can use the encrypted communication app Mark set up for us. It's secure."

They spent the next hour combing through the files, piecing together the connections between the various individuals involved in the operation. Eli felt a sense of urgency, knowing that every moment they delayed could put them further at risk.

As they worked, Eli couldn't shake the feeling that they were being watched. He glanced out the window, scanning the dark street outside. The quiet seemed oppressive, a warning of the storm that was brewing both literally and figuratively.

**A Sudden Change – 2:00 AM**
Just as they began to finalize their plan, the skies outside erupted in a torrential downpour. Rain pounded against the windows, and the wind howled, shaking the building.

"What a night," Cole remarked, glancing up at the stormy sky. "Do you think it's going to let up anytime soon?"

"It's going to be a long night," Carrie replied, her voice steady. "We'll just have to keep pushing through."

Eli felt a renewed sense of determination as they discussed their next steps. They needed to reach out to their contact, an investigative journalist named Emma, who had a reputation for exposing corruption.

"Let's get in touch with her," Eli said, opening the encrypted app on his phone. "She's our best shot at getting this information out."

As he typed out a message detailing their findings, the door to the inn suddenly creaked open, and a figure stepped inside, dripping wet from the rain.

"Eli? Is that you?" the figure called out, voice strained.

Eli's heart raced as he turned to see Emma, her face a mix of relief and concern. "You found me!" he exclaimed, rushing over.

"I saw your boat docked. I was worried you'd be followed," she said, glancing over her shoulder. "We need to talk, and fast."

Eli ushered her to the table, quickly explaining their situation. Emma listened intently, her expression shifting from surprise to determination as they shared the details of Operation Nightfall.

"This is big," she said, her eyes widening as she absorbed the information. "But we need to act quickly. If Faraday and Lincoln are as dangerous as you say, they won't hesitate to silence anyone who gets in their way."

"We know," Carrie replied, her voice steady. "That's why we're being cautious. We need to leak the information in a way that makes it undeniable."

Emma nodded, pulling out her own laptop. "Let's work together. I can get this information out to the right people and make sure it reaches the public."

As they collaborated, Eli felt a sense of urgency building. The storm outside mirrored the brewing conflict they were about to unleash. They had to move quickly, or the opportunity might slip away.

**Setting the Trap**

With Emma's expertise, they crafted a detailed article outlining the connections between Faraday, Lincoln, and their corrupt associates. Emma set up an anonymous tip line, ensuring their identities remained hidden.

"Once this goes public, they'll have no choice but to react," Emma explained, her fingers flying over the keyboard. "We'll create a media frenzy that forces law enforcement to get involved."

Eli watched as the pieces fell into place, the adrenaline pulsing through him. "We need to make sure to time the release just right, preferably when the media is most active."

"We can coordinate the release with the next news cycle," Emma suggested. "If we do it early in the morning, it'll catch them off guard."

As they finalized the article, the storm outside intensified, thunder rumbling ominously. Eli could feel the tension in the air, a sense that they were on the brink of something monumental.

"Okay," Eli said, taking a deep breath. "We're ready. Let's get this out there."

Carrie and Cole exchanged glances, a mix of excitement and fear evident in their eyes. They had come this far, and now it was time to make their stand.

As Emma clicked "send," a surge of hope filled the room. "It's done," she said, looking at each of them. "Now we wait."

## THE WAITING GAME

With the article sent, the group settled into a tense silence, the storm continuing to rage outside. The atmosphere was electric, filled with uncertainty and anticipation.

"Do you think they'll retaliate?" Cole asked, breaking the silence.

"I'm sure they will," Eli replied, his voice steady. "But we're ready for them. We'll stay vigilant."

As the hours passed, they kept an eye on the news, watching for any sign that their information had begun to circulate. The rain pounded against the roof, and the wind howled like a warning.

Suddenly, Eli's phone buzzed. He grabbed it, heart racing as he opened a news alert.

"Look!" he exclaimed, showing the screen to the group. "It's already breaking on multiple outlets!"

The headline read: **"Major Corruption Scandal Uncovered: Government Officials Linked to Crime Syndicate."**

Eli felt a rush of triumph. "They're in the spotlight now. This is just the beginning."

Carrie smiled, her eyes sparkling with determination. "We've got their attention. Now we need to stay ahead of them."

But as they celebrated their small victory, a deep rumble echoed through the building. Eli's heart sank.

"What was that?" Carrie asked, her smile fading.

"It sounded like it came from outside," Cole replied, moving toward the window.

Eli joined him, peering through the rain-soaked glass. In the distance, he could see flashing lights—police cars swarming the marina, their sirens piercing through the storm.

"They're moving," Eli said, dread creeping into his voice. "They're coming for us."

"Quick, we need to move!" Carrie urged, panic setting in.

Eli grabbed the laptop and phone, ready to leave. "Let's head out the back. We can slip through the woods."

As they made their way to the exit, the sound of footsteps grew louder, shouts echoing in the storm. The fight was far from over, and now the real danger was about to unfold.

**Into the Night**

Eli led the group through the back door, sprinting into the pouring rain. The storm enveloped them, the darkness making it hard to see, but they pressed on, adrenaline guiding their every step.

"Keep moving!" Eli shouted, glancing back at the inn. The flashing lights were getting closer, and he could hear the distant shouts of officers.

They plunged into the woods surrounding the inn, branches whipping against their skin as they ran deeper into the trees. The rain soaked them to the bone, but Eli didn't care. They had to find a way to escape.

"Where do we go?" Cole asked, breathless.

"There's a hunting cabin not far from here," Eli replied, his mind racing.

# Chapter 15: Into the Shadows

Eli led the way through the thick underbrush, the rain drenching their clothes and masking their footsteps. The sounds of the police search were muffled, but the tension in the air was palpable. They had to reach the hunting cabin before they were caught.

"Stay low and quiet," Eli instructed, glancing back to ensure everyone was following closely. The trees offered some cover, but they couldn't let their guard down.

"Do you think they'll track us?" Carrie asked, her voice barely above a whisper.

"Possibly," Eli replied, pushing through a thicket of branches. "But if we can make it to the cabin, we can lay low and figure out our next move."

As they navigated through the dense woods, Eli's mind raced with thoughts of Lincoln and Faraday. They were skilled and ruthless; the stakes were higher than ever. They couldn't afford to make a mistake.

After what felt like an eternity, Eli spotted the familiar silhouette of the hunting cabin nestled among the trees. "There it is!" he whispered urgently.

The group quickened their pace, finally reaching the cabin's door. Eli pushed it open cautiously, wincing as it creaked. The dim interior revealed a dusty, worn space filled with old furniture and remnants of past hunts.

"Looks abandoned," Cole said, peering inside. "Let's hope it stays that way."

Once inside, they quickly closed the door, leaning against it to catch their breath. The rain pounded on the roof, the sound soothing yet foreboding.

"Let's check the windows," Eli said, moving toward the grimy panes. "We need to know what's happening outside."

As he peered through the rain-streaked glass, Eli could see the glow of police flashlights cutting through the darkness. "They're searching the area," he muttered, heart pounding. "We need to keep quiet and stay hidden."

Carrie joined him, her eyes scanning the surroundings. "Do you think they'll come here?"

"If they suspect we're in the woods, they'll check every cabin," Eli replied, feeling the pressure mount. "We have to stay alert."

**Strategizing in the Dark**

They gathered in the center of the cabin, the air thick with tension. Eli opened the laptop, the glow illuminating their anxious faces.

"We need to decide our next move," he said, trying to focus. "We've exposed their operation, but they'll retaliate. We need a plan."

Carrie leaned forward. "What if we set a trap? We could use our leak to draw them out."

Eli considered this. "If we make it seem like we're about to expose more, it might lure them into the open. But we have to be careful. They're not just going to let us waltz in."

Cole rubbed his temples, looking stressed. "We need a backup plan. If things go south, we need to know how to escape."

Emma chimed in, glancing around the cabin. "I know the area pretty well. There's a network of old trails that can lead us to safety if we have to run."

"Good," Eli said, feeling a sense of relief wash over him. "If we can lure them into the open, we'll have a chance to escape through the trails."

They spent the next hour devising their strategy. Emma began drafting another message to send out anonymously, detailing their findings and hinting at a new lead that would keep the heat on Faraday and Lincoln.

"Once we send this, we need to prepare for whatever comes next," Eli instructed. "We'll have to be ready to move at a moment's notice."

Just as they finalized the message, a loud crash echoed outside, followed by shouts.

"They're here!" Carrie hissed, eyes wide with fear.

Eli's heart raced. "Everyone, stay low!"

They crouched behind the furniture as the door rattled. Footsteps approached, and Eli felt a cold sweat trickle down his back.

"Search the place!" a voice shouted, unmistakably Faraday's. "They can't have gone far!"

Eli held his breath, willing himself to stay calm. He glanced at Carrie, whose eyes mirrored his fear.

"Let's hope they don't check here," Cole whispered, tension thick in the air.

The door creaked open, and the beam of a flashlight swept across the room. Eli could see the silhouette of a figure standing in the doorway, peering inside.

**A Dangerous Game of Cat and Mouse**

Eli held his breath as Faraday stepped fully into the cabin, followed by a couple of guards. The light flickered over the dusty floorboards, illuminating the remnants of the old hunting cabin.

"Check behind the furniture!" Faraday commanded, scanning the room. "They can't hide forever."

Eli motioned for everyone to remain still, heart pounding in his ears. He felt the weight of their situation—one wrong move, and it could all be over.

As the guards began to search the cabin, Eli's mind raced. They had to create a diversion to escape.

"Emma," he whispered urgently, "do you have any ideas?"

She nodded, her eyes glinting with determination. "If I can find something to make noise outside, it might distract them long enough for us to slip out the back."

"Do it," Eli urged, glancing nervously at Faraday.

Emma slowly made her way toward the back door, careful not to make a sound. Eli held his breath as the guards continued to scour the cabin, their flashlight beams dancing across the walls.

Suddenly, Emma found an old canister of hunting supplies, knocking it to the ground. The loud clatter echoed through the cabin, drawing Faraday's attention.

"What was that?" Faraday shouted, turning toward the noise.

"Go!" Eli whispered urgently.

As the guards rushed to investigate, Eli motioned for Carrie and Cole to follow him out the back. They slipped through the door just as Faraday and the others turned their backs.

**Fleeing into the Storm**

Once outside, the rain pelted them relentlessly, but they didn't stop. Eli led them through the trees, their hearts racing as they sprinted away from the cabin and into the dark woods.

"Where do we go?" Carrie gasped, struggling to keep up.

"Follow me! There's a trail up ahead," Eli urged, adrenaline surging through him.

They pressed on, branches slapping against their arms and faces as they dashed deeper into the forest. Eli's mind raced with thoughts of the operation, their friends in danger, and the looming threat of Lincoln and Faraday.

After several minutes of running, they reached the old trail Emma had mentioned. It was narrow and overgrown, but it led away from the cabin and toward a series of hills.

"Keep moving," Eli said, his breath coming in quick bursts. "We have to put distance between us and them."

Just as they began to catch their breath, the sound of shouting echoed behind them. Faraday had realized they had escaped.

"They're coming!" Cole shouted, panic in his voice. "We need to hurry!"

Eli took the lead, pushing forward through the underbrush. The rain was relentless, but he felt a surge of determination. They couldn't let fear slow them down.

As they climbed the hill, the sound of footsteps behind them grew louder, and Eli felt the pressure mount. They had to reach the top before their pursuers caught up.

**The Turning Point**

At the summit, Eli paused, glancing back to see shadows moving through the trees. "We need a plan," he said, trying to catch his breath.

"Can we hide?" Carrie suggested, looking around for cover.

"There's a ravine over there," Emma pointed, her voice steady. "If we can get down there, we might be able to lose them."

"Let's go!" Eli urged, leading the way down the hill. They hurried toward the ravine, adrenaline pushing them forward.

As they reached the edge, Eli looked down at the steep drop. "It's a long way down. We need to be careful."

"Just go!" Cole urged, glancing back nervously.

One by one, they descended into the ravine, carefully navigating the slippery rocks. The rain continued to pour, turning the ground into a treacherous mudslide.

Eli felt a sense of urgency as they reached the bottom. "We need to find somewhere to hide."

They ducked behind a cluster of large boulders, their hearts racing. Eli listened intently, straining to hear any signs of their pursuers.

The sounds of shouts and splashes echoed through the rain-soaked air. "They're getting closer," Carrie whispered, fear evident in her voice.

"Just stay quiet," Eli urged, his heart pounding as they huddled together. "We can't let them find us."

The footsteps grew louder, the voices of Faraday and his guards echoing off the ravine walls. Eli felt his pulse quicken, and he knew they had to act fast.

Suddenly, a flashlight beam pierced through the rain, sweeping dangerously close to their hiding spot. Eli held his breath, praying they wouldn't be discovered.

"Split up!" Faraday's voice commanded, and Eli's heart sank. "They can't have gone far!"

**A Desperate Gambit**

Eli's mind raced as he considered their options. "If they split up, we can take them out one by one," he whispered to the group. "But we have to be strategic."

"Are you sure?" Carrie asked, her voice trembling.

"We don't have a choice. We can't let them catch us," Eli replied.

# Chapter 16: A Game of Survival

Eli scanned the dim ravine, his heart racing with the urgency of their situation. He knew they had to act quickly while the guards were split up, but the thought of confronting armed men made him uneasy.

"Here's the plan," Eli whispered, his voice low but firm. "We'll use the element of surprise. Emma and I will flank the first guard. Cole, you and Carrie create a distraction to draw the others away. Once we take him down, we'll regroup."

Carrie nodded, her eyes filled with determination. "I'll do whatever it takes."

Cole looked apprehensive but steeled himself. "Let's just hope we can handle them."

Eli crouched low, leading Emma to one side of the ravine while Carrie and Cole took the other. They could see the distant beam of a flashlight moving erratically as one of the guards searched for them.

"Stay close and be ready," Eli instructed Emma, glancing back to see Carrie and Cole in position. The rain continued to pour, masking their movements but also making the ground slick and treacherous.

As they positioned themselves, Eli spotted the first guard—he was alone, scanning the area, oblivious to their approach. Eli gestured to Emma, and they crept forward, their footsteps barely making a sound against the wet ground.

## THE CONFRONTATION

With a sudden burst of adrenaline, Eli and Emma sprang into action. Eli lunged at the guard from behind, tackling him to the ground. The man let out a surprised shout as they struggled, but Eli quickly got the upper hand, pinning him down.

Emma moved to help, securing the guard's arms behind his back. "Hurry!" Eli urged, glancing toward the path where the other guards were searching.

"Where are your friends?" Eli demanded, his voice low and fierce. "Tell me, and I won't hurt you."

The guard snarled, trying to break free. "You think this is over? You're dead meat!"

Eli's frustration boiled over, but he kept his composure. "You don't get it. If you don't talk, I'll make sure you wish you had."

Just then, a loud shout echoed from the other side of the ravine, signaling that Carrie and Cole had initiated their distraction.

"Now!" Eli yelled, and Emma helped him drag the guard behind the boulders, hiding him from view.

### The Distraction

Meanwhile, Carrie and Cole moved into position. They spotted another guard close by and decided to create a noise that would draw his attention.

"On three," Carrie whispered. "One... two... three!"

They threw rocks into the trees, creating a loud crash. The guard turned, alert, and began moving toward the sound, flashlight beam sweeping the area.

"Let's go!" Cole urged, his heart pounding as they followed the guard's movements.

As he approached the noise, Carrie gestured for Cole to flank him. They moved in sync, adrenaline fueling their courage.

The guard, distracted, didn't see them coming. Cole lunged, tackling the man from the side, while Carrie grabbed the guard's flashlight, using it to disorient him.

"Who are you?" the guard shouted, trying to push Cole off.

"Just a couple of friends," Cole said, determination in his voice. He quickly secured the guard's arms, immobilizing him.

"Nice work!" Carrie exclaimed, catching her breath. "Let's get him hidden before the others come back."

They dragged the guard behind a cluster of bushes, ensuring he wouldn't be seen.

**Regrouping**

Back in the ravine, Eli and Emma quickly tied up the first guard using the rope they had found in the cabin.

"Let's move before the others come back," Eli said, glancing nervously around. "We still have to deal with Faraday and whoever else is with him."

Emma nodded, looking at the guard they had subdued. "What should we do with him?"

"Leave him here for now," Eli decided. "We'll use him as leverage if we need to. Let's focus on finding the others and getting out of this alive."

They joined Carrie and Cole, who were catching their breath, adrenaline still surging through them.

"Two down, how many more?" Eli asked, scanning the surroundings.

"Just Faraday and one more," Carrie replied, her voice steady. "We can do this."

"Let's take them out before they can regroup," Eli urged. "We need to end this."

## The Final Stand

With their plan in place, the group moved silently through the ravine, each step calculated and precise. Eli led them toward the direction of the last two guards, his heart pounding in anticipation.

As they approached a clearing, Eli signaled for everyone to stop. He could see Faraday and the remaining guard ahead, standing under the dim light of a flashlight, debating their next move.

"Let's wait for them to split up," Eli whispered, watching intently. "Once they do, we'll strike."

Faraday seemed agitated, pacing as he spoke to the guard. "They can't have gone far! Spread out and find them!"

"Right," the guard replied, moving away from Faraday, who continued scanning the area.

"Now!" Eli urged, and they sprang into action.

Eli and Emma charged at Faraday, catching him off guard. Faraday reached for his weapon, but Eli was faster, tackling him to the ground. Emma quickly disarmed him, tossing the gun aside.

"Get down!" Cole shouted, tackling the other guard who had turned in response to the commotion. The two crashed to the ground, and Carrie jumped in to help.

## A Desperate Battle

As Eli struggled with Faraday, he could feel the man's strength. Faraday twisted and kicked, trying to gain the upper hand.

"Do you really think you can stop this?" Faraday spat, his eyes filled with venom. "You have no idea who you're dealing with."

Eli grunted, pressing down harder. "I know exactly who you are. And this is where it ends."

Meanwhile, Carrie and Cole grappled with the other guard, trying to keep him subdued. The fight was intense, but they worked together seamlessly, using their combined strength to gain the advantage.

"Get him! We can't let them escape!" Carrie yelled, determination driving her forward.

Eli felt the weight of Faraday's body beneath him. With one final push, he pinned the man down, panting heavily. "It's over."

As the struggle subsided, Cole and Carrie managed to subdue the remaining guard, and soon they had both men tied up securely.

**Facing the Truth**

With the immediate threat neutralized, Eli and his team took a moment to catch their breath. The storm still raged outside, but they felt a sense of accomplishment amidst the chaos.

"What now?" Carrie asked, her eyes flicking between the captured guards.

"We need to get them to a safe location," Emma suggested, looking at Eli. "They could help us expose the rest of the operation."

Eli nodded, feeling a mixture of relief and determination. "Agreed. But first, we need to find a way to contact the authorities without putting ourselves at risk."

They quickly devised a plan, using the guards' phones to send a message to their contact within law enforcement. They couldn't risk being traced back to the incident, so they made sure to erase any signs of their involvement.

As they finished their preparations, Eli couldn't shake the feeling that they were still in danger. Faraday and Lincoln would be relentless, and they had to remain vigilant.

"Let's move," Eli said, leading the way back through the ravine, the sound of the rain masking their escape. "We still have a long way to go."

**The Road Ahead**

As they reached the edge of the woods, the sound of sirens began to echo in the distance, getting closer. Eli felt a rush of hope—help was on the way.

"Over here!" he shouted, waving his arms. "We're here!"

The headlights of several police cars pierced through the rain, illuminating the clearing. Officers spilled out, rushing toward them.

"Are you all right?" one officer called, scanning the group.

"Yes, we captured them," Eli said, gesturing to the tied-up guards. "They were part of a larger operation. We have evidence."

The officers quickly took control, securing the guards and assessing the situation. Eli felt a sense of relief wash over him as they handed over the information they had gathered.

As the rain began to let up, Eli exchanged glances with Carrie, Cole, and Emma. They had faced the storm together, and they had emerged stronger.

But Eli knew this was just the beginning. Lincoln and Faraday would not go down without a fight, and their battle was far from over.

"Whatever happens next, we face it together," Eli said, determination flooding his voice.

With the dawn breaking on the horizon, they stood united, ready to confront the challenges ahead. The fight for justice had just begun.

# Chapter 17: After the Storm

The rain had subsided, leaving a thick mist hanging in the air as the first rays of dawn broke through the trees. Eli stood with Carrie, Cole, and Emma, watching as the police secured the area and took statements from the captured guards. Relief washed over him, but an undercurrent of anxiety remained. The threat of Lincoln loomed large in his mind.

"Are you sure they'll stay put?" Carrie asked, her eyes darting toward the officers as they worked.

Eli nodded, though he couldn't shake the feeling that this was only a temporary reprieve. "Faraday and Lincoln are resourceful. They'll find a way to retaliate if they get the chance."

Emma, standing nearby, glanced at Eli, concern etched on her face. "What's our next step? We can't just sit back and wait for them to strike."

Eli took a deep breath, feeling the weight of their situation. "We need to expose their entire operation. If we can gather enough evidence and get it to the media, we might be able to take them down for good."

**Building the Case**

Once the police finished taking their statements, Eli and his friends were taken to a nearby station for their protection and to provide a more detailed account of what had transpired. After what felt like an eternity, they finally sat down with an investigator named Officer Daniels, who had a no-nonsense demeanor.

"Tell me everything," Daniels said, leaning forward, pen poised over his notebook.

Eli recounted their discovery of the operation, the threats they faced, and their confrontation with Faraday and the guards. Each detail was met with nods of understanding from Officer Daniels, who seemed to recognize the gravity of the situation.

"This is bigger than I thought," Daniels said, running a hand through his hair. "We'll need all the evidence you can provide. If Lincoln and Faraday are connected to a larger crime syndicate, we can't let them slip through our fingers."

Carrie chimed in, "We have information from a confidential source about their transactions and locations. If we can get that to you, it might help build a stronger case."

"Good," Daniels said. "I'll have my team work on this immediately. In the meantime, I suggest you all stay somewhere safe. They might come looking for you."

**Finding Refuge**

After the meeting, Eli and his friends were given temporary housing in a safe house while they waited for updates. It was a small, unassuming cabin on the outskirts of town, far removed from their usual haunts.

As they settled in, Eli felt a sense of camaraderie among them. "We've made it this far," he said, trying to lift the mood. "Let's keep the momentum going."

Carrie smiled weakly. "We'll figure this out. Together."

Days passed as they huddled in the safe house, working tirelessly to compile evidence and prepare their findings. They connected with their anonymous source, who provided crucial documents and information about Lincoln's network.

But every passing day heightened Eli's anxiety. The fear of what Lincoln might do to silence them loomed over him like a dark cloud.

## A SHOCKING REVELATION

One evening, as they were poring over documents, Emma suddenly looked up, her expression grave. "I just got a text from our source. Lincoln knows we're still alive. He's mobilizing his team to find us."

Eli's heart sank. "How does he know?"

"I don't know, but we have to act fast," Emma said, her hands shaking. "We can't let him get to us first."

"Then we need to send everything we have to the police now," Eli said, urgency rising in his voice. "They need to be prepared for whatever Lincoln is planning."

As they gathered their materials, the tension in the air grew thick. Eli felt the weight of responsibility pressing down on him. They were running out of time.

Suddenly, a loud bang echoed outside, causing them all to jump.

"What was that?" Carrie whispered, her eyes wide with fear.

"Stay quiet," Eli instructed, his heart racing as he moved toward the window.

### The Attack

Peering through the misty glass, Eli's stomach dropped. A black SUV was parked outside, and he could see figures moving stealthily toward the cabin.

"Get down!" he shouted, diving for cover just as a barrage of gunfire shattered the tranquility of the safe house.

"Eli!" Cole yelled, panic evident in his voice.

"Stay low!" Eli ordered, scrambling to the back of the cabin. They needed to find a way to escape before it was too late.

"Do you have a plan?" Emma asked, fear flashing in her eyes.

"I'll create a diversion," Eli said, looking for anything that could help. He spotted a heavy metal toolbox in the corner. "I'll make noise to draw them away. You guys need to get to the back exit and head for the woods."

Carrie shook her head. "We can't leave you!"

"This isn't a debate," Eli replied firmly. "You have to trust me. We'll meet back at the rendezvous point if I can buy you some time."

"Okay," Cole said reluctantly. "Just be careful."

Eli nodded, steeling himself. He had to make this count.

**A Dangerous Gamble**

Eli grabbed the toolbox and moved to the front of the cabin, taking a deep breath. With a quick heave, he threw the toolbox outside, where it landed with a loud crash.

"Hey! Over here!" he shouted, trying to draw their attention.

As he expected, the figures turned, and Eli saw the glint of weapons. Heart pounding, he sprinted toward the back exit, hoping to create enough of a distraction for his friends to escape.

Outside, the assailants rushed toward the noise, and Eli slipped through the back door, adrenaline fueling his every move. He made his way toward the treeline, ducking low to avoid detection.

As he reached the edge of the woods, he turned to see if his friends had made it out.

Just then, a shout echoed behind him. "There he is! Get him!"

**Into the Woods**

Eli bolted into the forest, the sound of footsteps pounding behind him. He could hear the shouts growing closer, but he had to keep moving.

Branches whipped against his face as he navigated through the underbrush, desperate to put distance between himself and the attackers. His heart raced, and he could feel panic creeping in, but he fought to stay focused.

"Think, Eli, think!" he muttered to himself as he darted between trees. He needed a plan—a place to hide until he could regroup with the others.

Suddenly, he spotted a large fallen tree trunk ahead. He quickly ducked behind it, catching his breath and trying to calm his racing heart.

Peering through the underbrush, he watched as two figures passed by, searching the area. Eli held his breath, hoping they wouldn't see him.

Once they moved further away, Eli knew he had to find his friends. He could only hope they had escaped the cabin safely.

**A Daring Reunion**

After several tense moments, Eli cautiously made his way back toward the direction of the safe house, staying low and quiet. The rain had stopped, but the air was thick with tension.

As he approached the cabin, he spotted movement among the trees. "Carrie? Cole? Emma?" he called softly, praying they were okay.

A moment later, Carrie emerged from the shadows, breathless and wide-eyed. "Eli! We thought we lost you!"

"I'm fine," he replied, relief flooding through him. "Where are Cole and Emma?"

"They're safe. We managed to hide out of sight until the attackers left," she said, glancing back toward the cabin. "We need to get out of here. They'll come back."

"Agreed," Eli said, scanning the area for any signs of danger. "Do you know the way to the rendezvous point?"

"Yes, I marked it on the map earlier," Carrie replied, pulling it out. "But we need to move quickly."

They quickly gathered their belongings and headed deeper into the woods, each step fueled by a mix of fear and determination. They couldn't let Lincoln and Faraday win.

## THE PATH FORWARD

As they navigated the dense forest, Eli felt a renewed sense of purpose. They had faced danger together, and each challenge had only made them stronger.

"We're going to finish this," Eli said, glancing at Carrie. "We're going to expose them once and for all."

Carrie nodded, her eyes shining with determination. "We can't let them control our lives anymore."

They pressed on, navigating the underbrush with urgency. The weight of their mission hung heavy in the air, but they were united in their resolve.

As they finally reached the rendezvous point, Eli knew they had a long road ahead of them. But with his friends by his side, he felt ready to face whatever came next.

The fight was just beginning, and they wouldn't back down.

# Chapter 18: The Calm Before the Storm

The rendezvous point was a secluded clearing deep in the woods, a place Eli had scouted weeks earlier. The sun dipped low on the horizon, casting long shadows as they gathered around a small campfire. Tension hung in the air, but a flicker of hope ignited with the flames.

"Are we sure this is safe?" Cole asked, glancing around nervously. "What if they find us here?"

Eli looked around, considering their surroundings. "This is the best we could do for now. It's secluded, and the trees provide cover. But we have to stay alert."

Emma, sitting close to the fire, pulled out her phone. "I've been trying to reach Officer Daniels for updates. We need to know what they're doing with the information we provided."

"Let's hope they're moving fast," Carrie said, rubbing her arms against the evening chill. "Lincoln won't waste time trying to find us again."

As they settled in, Eli spread out the maps and documents they had gathered. "We need to create a timeline of their operations and figure out who else is involved. If we can identify key players, we can make a stronger case."

The group nodded, their focus shifting to the task at hand. Eli outlined their findings, marking locations and connections on the map, piecing together the puzzle of Lincoln's operation.

## A Dark Discovery

Hours passed as they worked under the glow of the campfire, but as they delved deeper, Eli felt a growing unease. Something was off.

"Look at this," he said, pointing to a set of documents that Emma had unearthed. "These transactions aren't just local. They extend to other states, even overseas."

Carrie leaned in, squinting at the papers. "This is bigger than we thought. If they have connections like this... we might be dealing with a larger syndicate."

Cole sighed, running a hand through his hair. "So, what do we do? We can't take this on by ourselves."

Eli felt the weight of their situation. "We need to get this information to the authorities and make sure they take it seriously. But we have to be careful. Lincoln's men will be looking for us."

Suddenly, Emma's phone buzzed. "It's Officer Daniels!" she exclaimed, answering it quickly.

"Eli, we need to talk," Daniels said, his voice tense on the other end. "We've got intel that Lincoln is planning something big. We believe he might come after you directly."

Eli's stomach twisted. "What do you mean?"

"There's been chatter about a shipment that could involve your location. We think they're going to use it as a distraction to find you. You need to move, and fast."

"Where should we go?" Eli asked, his mind racing.

"Head to the old barn on Mill Creek Road. It's abandoned and should be out of their radar for now. I'll send backup as soon as I can," Daniels instructed.

"Understood. We're on our way," Eli said, hanging up and turning to his friends. "We need to go—now."

### A Race Against Time

Panic surged through the group as they packed their belongings, urgency propelling them into action. The night was dark, and the forest felt ominous as they retraced their steps toward Mill Creek Road.

"Do you think we'll make it?" Emma asked, her voice barely above a whisper.

"We have to," Eli replied, determination firming his resolve. "If Lincoln's planning something, we need to get to that barn before it happens."

As they moved swiftly through the woods, the sound of branches snapping underfoot echoed in the stillness. Eli's heart raced with every sound, aware that danger could be lurking just out of sight.

"Keep quiet and stick close," he instructed, leading the way.

Suddenly, a flash of headlights pierced the darkness ahead. Eli froze, instinctively pulling everyone to the side.

"Is that them?" Carrie whispered, her eyes wide.

"I can't tell," Eli replied, squinting into the distance. "But we can't risk it."

They ducked behind a thick cluster of trees, holding their breath as the vehicle approached. The SUV rolled to a stop not far from where they hid, and a group of shadowy figures emerged, talking in hushed tones.

"Stay here," Eli instructed, peering through the foliage. "Let's see what they're up to."

### The Encounter

As the figures began to move away from the vehicle, Eli's heart sank. He recognized one of them—it was Faraday. The men were armed, scanning the area with flashlights, clearly on the hunt.

"Split up," Faraday ordered. "We'll cover more ground this way. If they're here, they can't have gone far."

Eli's pulse quickened. They needed to get to the barn and fast. He turned to his friends, whispering urgently. "We have to make a break for it. We can't let them find us here."

"Are you sure?" Cole asked, his eyes darting nervously.

"Now or never," Eli replied, steeling himself. "On my count."

As Eli began to count down, the figures started to move closer. "Three... two... one... go!"

They burst from the trees, sprinting toward the barn as fast as they could. Eli could hear the shouts of the men behind them, their footsteps pounding the ground.

**The Barn**

They reached the old barn, its weathered wood creaking under the weight of their hurried entry. Eli pushed the door closed, pressing against it to hold it shut as they caught their breath.

"Did we lose them?" Emma panted, her eyes wide with fear.

"For now," Eli replied, scanning the dim interior. "We need to find a place to hide until backup arrives."

The barn was dark and filled with debris, but Eli spotted a pile of hay bales in the corner. "Over there!" he whispered, leading them to the makeshift hiding spot.

As they crouched down, Eli strained to hear any sounds outside. The muffled shouts of Faraday's crew grew distant, but the anxiety in his chest wouldn't subside.

**A Plan in the Shadows**

As they settled in, Eli turned to the group. "We need to formulate a plan for when help arrives. If Lincoln knows we're here, we can't let our guard down."

Carrie nodded, glancing at the door. "What if they try to come inside? We need to be prepared."

"We could block the door with something heavy," Cole suggested, looking around. "There's some old equipment over there."

"Good idea," Eli said, and they all quietly moved to gather anything they could use to barricade the entrance.

As they worked, Eli felt a rush of determination. They had come too far to back down now. Together, they could outsmart Lincoln and his crew.

**Time is Running Out**

Once they had barricaded the door, Eli looked at his friends, each of them breathing heavily but focused. "We need to stay alert. If they find us, it won't end well."

Emma pulled out her phone again, but there was no signal. "I can't reach Officer Daniels. We're completely cut off."

"That's okay," Eli reassured her. "We'll hold our ground until back-up arrives."

Minutes felt like hours as they waited in the dim light of the barn, their breaths synchronized with the sound of the wind rustling outside.

Suddenly, the sound of footsteps echoed outside the barn. Eli's heart raced as he strained to listen.

"Search the barn!" a voice called out.

Faraday's men had found them.

"Get ready," Eli whispered, his pulse quickening. "They'll try to get in."

As the footsteps drew closer, Eli prepared himself for the confrontation that was about to unfold. They had fought too hard to let fear take hold now. Together, they would face whatever came next.

# Chapter 19: The Confrontation

The sound of footsteps grew louder as Faraday's men approached the barn. Eli's heart raced, his mind racing with strategies for what to do next. He could feel the tension in the air, thick and suffocating.

"Stay quiet," he whispered, glancing at his friends. "If they get in, we need to stick together."

As they huddled behind the hay bales, the heavy door creaked, and Eli held his breath. A moment later, it burst open, and a beam of light from a flashlight cut through the darkness.

"Check the corners!" a voice ordered, and Eli's stomach dropped. They were in trouble.

"Here!" one of the men shouted, pointing toward the hay. "They're hiding!"

"Get in there!" Faraday's voice boomed from outside. "We're not leaving until we find them!"

Eli's mind raced as he tried to devise a plan. "We need a distraction," he said, low and urgent. "Something to pull them away from us."

"Like what?" Emma asked, her voice trembling.

Eli scanned the barn, searching for anything that could help. His eyes landed on an old gas canister tucked in a corner. "If we can create a small fire or a loud noise, it might buy us some time to escape."

"Are you sure that's safe?" Cole whispered, doubt lacing his voice.

"It's a risk we have to take," Eli replied, his resolve hardening. "I'll do it."

**The Plan in Action**

Eli carefully crept toward the canister, trying to make as little noise as possible. He could hear the men outside growing impatient, their footsteps stomping around the perimeter of the barn.

"Where the hell are they?" one of them muttered.

Eli reached the canister, his heart pounding. He fumbled for a lighter in his pocket, hoping it would still work. With a quick flick, the flame ignited, and he felt a rush of adrenaline.

"Now!" he hissed, as he poured a small amount of gas onto some hay scattered nearby, keeping a safe distance from the canister itself.

The flames caught quickly, and Eli shoved the canister toward the far end of the barn, where it landed with a thud.

"Look out!" he yelled, drawing the attention of the men outside.

**Chaos Unleashed**

The sound of the fire crackling echoed through the barn as the flames spread. The men outside reacted with alarm, rushing toward the entrance.

"Get back! It's going to explode!" one shouted.

Eli turned to his friends, urgency flashing in his eyes. "Now's our chance! Let's go!"

They bolted toward the back of the barn, where a small window was partially open. Eli hoisted Emma up, and she squeezed through, landing silently on the other side.

"Go! I'll help Cole," Eli urged, turning to lift his friend.

Just as Cole scrambled through, an explosion rocked the barn, sending debris flying. Eli ducked, narrowly avoiding a shower of wood and hay.

"Go! Get to the woods!" he shouted, pushing Cole and Emma ahead.

## INTO THE NIGHT

Eli followed them out into the cool night air, the flames illuminating the clearing behind them. The chaotic sounds of shouting and confusion filled the air as Faraday's men scrambled to deal with the unexpected fire.

"Keep moving!" Eli yelled, urging his friends deeper into the woods.

They sprinted away from the barn, adrenaline surging as they navigated the darkness. Eli's mind raced with thoughts of escape and survival, each heartbeat echoing in his ears.

"Where to now?" Carrie panted, glancing back toward the growing fire.

"We need to find a place to hide until backup arrives," Eli replied, scanning the trees for cover. "Let's head toward the creek. We can lose them in the water."

They continued running, their breaths heavy as they pushed forward, the sounds of the fire fading behind them.

### A Brief Respite

After what felt like an eternity, they reached the creek. The water rushed over the rocks, cool and inviting, but the threat was still real.

"Let's take a moment," Eli said, trying to catch his breath. "We'll need to regroup and come up with our next move."

As they crouched by the water, they could hear the distant sounds of the commotion from the barn. The fire crackled, but it was a temporary distraction; Lincoln's men would regroup soon.

"Do you think they'll find us?" Emma asked, her voice shaky.

"We need to be smart," Eli replied, his mind racing. "They'll assume we're trying to get away, but we can't run forever. We need to turn the tables."

"Turn the tables?" Carrie repeated, her brow furrowed. "How?"

"If we can lure them into a trap, we might have a chance to catch them off guard," Eli said, formulating a plan. "We need to make it look like we're vulnerable, but we'll be ready."

**The Trap**

Eli explained his idea, and his friends listened intently. They could use the creek's natural features to their advantage, setting up a diversion that would draw the men away while they prepared an ambush.

"Let's use some branches and leaves to create a false trail," Eli suggested. "If we can make it look like we're heading downstream, they'll follow that way."

"Then what?" Cole asked, his brows knitted together.

"While they're busy chasing us down the creek, we'll set up an ambush on the opposite bank. If they think they have us cornered, we'll catch them by surprise."

With a shared sense of purpose, they began to work quickly, gathering branches and debris to mask their movements. They moved stealthily along the creek, leaving behind a trail that would lead the men away.

**The Moment of Truth**

Once they finished, Eli glanced around, feeling the weight of the moment. "This is it. We need to stick to the plan and be ready."

As they hid behind a cluster of trees, they heard the sound of footsteps approaching. Eli's heart raced, adrenaline coursing through him.

"Spread out and search the area!" a voice barked, unmistakably Faraday's.

"Stay low," Eli whispered, holding his breath as the men came into view.

They were on the opposite bank, scanning the creek for signs of movement. Eli could see the tension in his friends' faces, but he knew they had to remain focused.

"Now!" he whispered, motioning for them to get ready.

Just as the men turned their backs, Eli and his friends sprang into action, charging out from their hiding spots and shouting as they charged toward the unsuspecting group.

## THE AMBUSH

Surprise painted the faces of Faraday's men as Eli and his friends launched their ambush. Eli tackled the nearest man, taking him by surprise as they crashed to the ground.

"Get them!" Faraday shouted, trying to regain control, but chaos erupted as Eli's friends joined the fray, each one fighting with determination.

Cole wrestled with one of the guards, while Carrie took on another, using everything they had learned in their training. Emma stayed close to Eli, her eyes fierce with resolve.

In the midst of the struggle, Eli caught a glimpse of Faraday, his expression one of fury. "You think you can defeat us? This is only the beginning!"

Eli felt a rush of anger. "You won't hurt anyone else!" he shouted, focusing on the fight.

With each punch thrown and every move executed, Eli felt the tide shifting. They had the upper hand, fueled by their desire for justice and survival.

### A Turning Point

As the fight intensified, Eli spotted an opening. He maneuvered past the scuffle to confront Faraday directly. "This ends here!" he yelled, charging forward.

Faraday laughed derisively, raising his weapon. "You think you can take me down?"

Eli lunged, using all his strength to tackle Faraday to the ground. They rolled in the dirt, the struggle for dominance fierce. Eli could feel the man's strength, but he knew he couldn't give up.

"Get off him!" Carrie shouted, tackling another guard who was approaching Eli from behind.

Eli managed to pin Faraday down, his hands gripping the man's shoulders. "This is for everyone you've hurt!"

Just then, the sound of sirens pierced the night, growing louder as they approached.

**The Endgame**

With the sound of approaching police cars, the remaining guards began to panic. "We need to go!" one shouted, scrambling to get to their vehicle.

"Not so fast!" Cole yelled, lunging to block their path.

In the chaos, Eli held Faraday down, his breath heavy with exertion. "You're not going anywhere."

"Let me go!" Faraday snarled, struggling against Eli's grip.

But Eli's resolve was unyielding. "You're done. Your operation is over."

As the police arrived, lights flashing, they quickly took control of the situation, apprehending Faraday's men one by one.

"Eli! Are you okay?" Officer Daniels called out, rushing to their side.

"We're fine," Eli replied, releasing Faraday, who was now surrounded by law enforcement.

The weight of the fight began to lift as the police secured the area, and Eli felt a rush of relief. They had done it. They had fought back and won.

# Chapter 20: A New Dawn After the Battle

As dawn broke, painting the sky with hues of orange and pink, Eli and his friends stood by the creek, watching as the police secured the area. Relief washed over him, but it was mixed with the exhaustion of the battle they had just fought.

"Is it really over?" Emma asked, her voice trembling slightly as she took in the sight of Faraday being led away in handcuffs.

"For now," Eli replied, trying to steady his own heartbeat. "But we have to stay vigilant. There are still unanswered questions about Lincoln and the larger operation."

Officer Daniels approached them, a serious expression on his face. "I need to commend you all for your bravery. What you did back there could have turned out very differently. You gave us the intel we needed."

Eli felt a swell of pride. "We couldn't let them get away with it. We had to fight back."

Daniels nodded, glancing at the remnants of the battle. "We're going to need your testimonies and all the evidence you gathered. This is just the beginning of dismantling their operation."

Carrie spoke up, her voice strong. "We're ready to help in any way we can. We can't let them hurt anyone else."

"Good. I'll have my team compile everything, but first, you all need to take a moment. You've been through a lot," Daniels replied, gesturing toward the police vehicles.

### A Moment of Reflection

As they moved away from the chaos, Eli found a quiet spot by the creek, away from the officers and the noise of the gathering crowd. His friends joined him, and for a moment, they simply breathed.

"I can't believe we made it," Cole said, shaking his head in disbelief. "That was insane."

Eli nodded, still trying to process everything that had happened. "We did what we had to do. But I'm just glad we're all okay."

Emma looked at him, her expression a mix of gratitude and concern. "Eli, you were incredible. I don't think we could've done it without you."

"I couldn't have done it without all of you," Eli replied earnestly. "We fought together. That made the difference."

Carrie smiled softly. "We're a team. And no matter what happens next, we'll face it together."

### The Fallout

As the sun climbed higher, the reality of what lay ahead settled over them. Officer Daniels approached again, this time with a clipboard in hand.

"Are you all ready to give your statements?" he asked.

Eli nodded. "We're ready. Let's do this."

They each took turns recounting their experiences, detailing everything from their initial discovery of the operation to the ambush by the creek. It was cathartic, finally putting their experiences into words and knowing they were helping to bring justice.

Afterward, Eli stepped outside, needing a moment to breathe. He spotted Faraday being loaded into a police car, his expression dark and furious. Their eyes met, and Eli felt a shiver run down his spine.

"You think this is the end, don't you?" Faraday shouted, his voice filled with malice. "You have no idea what you're up against."

Eli swallowed hard, the weight of Faraday's words settling in. "We'll stop you. We won't let you hurt anyone else."

"Good luck with that," Faraday sneered before being shut inside the vehicle.

### The Path Ahead

As the police began to disperse, Eli and his friends reconvened, still feeling the adrenaline coursing through them.

"What now?" Cole asked, glancing around. "Do we just wait for them to take down Lincoln and his operation?"

Eli took a deep breath, contemplating their next steps. "We'll have to stay involved. This isn't over until we're sure everyone is held accountable. Lincoln won't stop easily, especially after this."

"Then we'll keep fighting," Carrie said, her determination shining through. "We can't let fear dictate our lives anymore."

Emma nodded, her voice steady. "We need to keep gathering evidence and staying in touch with Officer Daniels. If there are more people involved, we have to find them."

Eli felt a renewed sense of purpose. "Exactly. We're not just victims anymore. We're part of the solution."

### A New Beginning

As they stood by the creek, watching the sun rise higher, Eli felt a shift within himself. They had faced darkness together and emerged stronger.

"Let's promise to stay united, no matter what," he said, looking each of them in the eye.

"Absolutely," Emma said, a smile breaking through her earlier tension.

"Together," Cole affirmed, raising his hand.

"Together," Carrie echoed, placing her hand on top of his.

Eli added his hand to the pile, feeling a sense of belonging and strength. "Together."

With that simple word, they forged a pact—one that would see them through whatever challenges lay ahead.

As they walked back toward the police vehicles, Eli felt a weight lift from his shoulders. The fight was far from over, but they were ready for whatever came next. With determination in their hearts, they stepped into the future, united and resolute.

# Chapter 21: The Investigation Deepens

In the days that followed the confrontation at the creek, Eli and his friends settled into a new routine. The police had launched a full investigation into Lincoln's operation, but Eli knew they couldn't sit idly by. Their involvement was crucial in piecing together the larger puzzle.

"Let's meet at my place after school," Eli suggested one afternoon, gathering everyone at his house. "We need to strategize and stay on top of what's happening."

As they gathered in Eli's living room, the air was charged with a mix of anticipation and anxiety. They spread out maps and documents across the coffee table, trying to connect the dots of Lincoln's syndicate.

"Officer Daniels said the intel we provided was solid, but we need more specifics," Emma said, pointing to a section of the map. "What if we focus on the locations tied to those transactions?"

"Good idea," Carrie replied, pulling out her laptop. "I can cross-reference these locations with any recent police reports or suspicious activity."

Cole leaned in, tracing his finger along the map. "If we can identify more people in Lincoln's circle, we might be able to disrupt their operations further."

Eli nodded, feeling a surge of determination. "Let's divide the locations and start digging. We can meet up tomorrow to share our findings."

## A NEW LEAD

The next day at school, Eli couldn't shake the feeling of being watched. He glanced around the hallways, his senses heightened. Though everything appeared normal, an undercurrent of tension lingered.

As the bell rang, Eli and his friends gathered in a secluded corner of the cafeteria, spreading out their findings.

"I found something interesting," Emma said, her eyes wide with excitement. "This location here," she pointed to the map, "matches up with a shipping yard that's had multiple complaints about suspicious activity."

"Shipping yard?" Cole echoed, intrigued. "That could be a key part of Lincoln's operation. If they're moving goods through there, we might uncover a larger network."

Eli felt a mix of excitement and apprehension. "If we decide to check it out, we need to be careful. We don't want to put ourselves in danger again."

"Agreed," Carrie said, her expression serious. "But if we can gather evidence, it could help bring down Lincoln for good."

Eli nodded, a plan forming in his mind. "Let's scope it out tonight. We can go in under the cover of darkness and see what we can find."

**The Night Mission**

As night fell, Eli and his friends gathered at the edge of the shipping yard, the dim lights casting eerie shadows across the lot. The air was thick with tension, but their resolve remained firm.

"Stay close and keep your voices down," Eli instructed, leading the way. "We don't want to attract attention."

They moved stealthily, using the containers for cover as they crept deeper into the yard. The sounds of machinery and distant voices created an unsettling backdrop, heightening their senses.

"Over there," Emma whispered, pointing to a cluster of containers at the far end of the lot. "That's where the reports mentioned unusual activity."

Eli nodded, gesturing for them to follow. As they approached, he could see figures moving in the shadows, their hushed voices indistinct.

"Let's listen," Carrie suggested, crouching behind a nearby container.

**Eavesdropping**

Peering around the edge, they caught sight of a small group of men gathered near a large shipping container, their body language tense.

"We need to move this shipment out by tomorrow," one of them said, his voice low and urgent. "If Lincoln finds out we're delayed, heads will roll."

"What about the girls?" another man asked. "They're still a problem. We can't afford to have them snooping around."

Eli's heart raced. They were talking about them. About their fight against Lincoln.

"We'll handle it," the first man replied, glancing around. "Just focus on getting this shipment ready. We can deal with the kids later."

Eli exchanged worried glances with his friends. They needed to act fast before the men became aware of their presence.

**The Plan of Action**

"Let's get out of here and report this to Officer Daniels," Eli whispered urgently. "This is our chance to bring down more of Lincoln's operation."

As they turned to leave, a sudden noise startled them—a clattering sound as one of the men bumped into a stack of crates.

"Did you hear that?" the man called out, his voice rising with alarm.

Eli's heart raced as he and his friends ducked behind a nearby container, holding their breath as the men approached.

"Search the area!" one of them shouted, their urgency palpable. "We can't let anyone find out what we're doing!"

## A NARROW ESCAPE

Panic surged through Eli as he realized they were being hunted. "We need to move, now!" he urged, motioning for his friends to follow him.

They dashed away from the containers, sprinting toward the edge of the yard. The sounds of footsteps followed closely behind, growing louder.

"Over there!" one of the men shouted, spotting them.

Eli pushed his legs to run faster, his breath coming in ragged gasps. "This way!" he yelled, leading them toward a gap in the fence.

They barely squeezed through, the sound of shouting behind them urging them on.

"Keep going!" Carrie shouted, and they didn't look back until they reached the cover of the trees.

**Regrouping**

Once they were safely hidden, they paused to catch their breath, hearts pounding in their chests.

"That was way too close," Cole gasped, leaning against a tree.

Eli nodded, adrenaline still coursing through him. "But we got valuable information. We need to get back to Officer Daniels and report what we heard."

"Let's head to my house," Emma suggested. "We can make a plan from there."

As they hurried back, Eli felt a renewed sense of purpose. They had faced danger, but they were still standing together. Whatever it took, they would uncover the truth and stop Lincoln's operation once and for all.

## THE FINAL PUSH

Once they reached Emma's house, they settled around her kitchen table, the urgency of their mission still fresh in their minds.

"Let's break down what we heard," Eli said, spreading the notes they had taken. "We know there's a shipment coming in, and it's crucial that we alert Officer Daniels immediately."

Emma grabbed her phone, quickly dialing Daniels' number. "We have to make him understand how serious this is," she said as the phone rang.

"Eli, what if they find out we're the ones who tipped him off?" Carrie asked, anxiety creeping into her voice.

"We can't let fear control us. We have to act," Eli replied, determination hardening his resolve.

**A Critical Decision**

When Officer Daniels finally answered, Eli wasted no time. "Daniels, we have critical information about Lincoln's operation. There's a shipment scheduled for tomorrow, and we overheard them talking about us. They know we're involved."

"Where are you now?" Daniels asked, his tone shifting to urgency.

"Emma's house," Eli replied. "We can meet there and provide all the details."

"Stay put. I'll be there as soon as I can," Daniels said before hanging up.

"Now we wait," Emma said, glancing at the clock.

They spent the next hour reviewing their notes, anxiety building with every passing minute. Each tick of the clock felt like a countdown.

Finally, they heard the sound of tires crunching on gravel outside.

"Is that him?" Cole asked, peering out the window.

"Looks like it," Eli said, feeling a surge of hope. "Let's make sure we have everything ready to present."

As they gathered their notes, Eli felt a sense of camaraderie wash over them. They were in this together, and no matter the outcome, they had each other's backs.

When Officer Daniels entered, he quickly assessed the situation, his expression serious.

"Let's hear what you've got," he said, taking a seat at the table.

Eli took a deep breath, ready to deliver everything they had uncovered. They were on the brink of making a difference, and nothing would stand in their way.

# Chapter 22: The Final Countdown

As Eli and his friends presented their findings to Officer Daniels, the atmosphere in the room was charged with urgency. They laid out the details of what they had overheard and mapped out the potential locations involved in Lincoln's operation.

"From what you've told me, this shipment could be a major turning point in taking down the entire network," Daniels said, his expression grave. "We need to act quickly."

Eli leaned forward, his heart pounding. "Do you have a plan?"

Daniels nodded, pulling out a folder filled with information. "We're organizing a raid on the shipping yard. Your intel will help us pinpoint exactly what to target."

"Can we be involved?" Emma asked, a determined look in her eyes. "We've already put ourselves in danger; we want to see this through."

Daniels hesitated, weighing the risks. "I appreciate your bravery, but this operation will be risky. We can't guarantee your safety."

"We can handle it," Cole said, his voice steady. "We've faced danger before. We want to help put an end to this."

After a moment of silence, Daniels sighed. "Alright. You can be involved, but under strict conditions. You'll stay back and provide support. We don't want to put you in direct danger again."

Eli felt a rush of adrenaline. "We're in. Whatever it takes to bring Lincoln down."

## THE OPERATION

As night fell, the group prepared for the raid. Officer Daniels briefed the team, emphasizing the importance of caution and communication. Eli's heart raced with a mix of excitement and fear.

"Remember, we're working together," Daniels reminded them. "Stay close to your radios and keep an eye out."

They arrived at the shipping yard, the air thick with tension. Eli, Emma, Carrie, and Cole set up in a nearby van, ready to relay information and observe the operation.

Through the van's windows, they watched as police vehicles moved into position, officers moving with practiced precision.

"Here we go," Eli whispered, adrenaline coursing through him. The moment of truth had arrived.

The operation began. Officers advanced toward the yard, surrounding it silently. Eli could see the shadows of the men they had overheard earlier, moving nervously near the shipping container.

"Stay alert," Emma said, her eyes glued to the scene outside.

Suddenly, an explosion of noise erupted as the police moved in, shouting commands and catching the men by surprise. The chaos unfolded quickly, and Eli felt a surge of hope.

**The Showdown**

As officers closed in on the criminals, Eli and his friends monitored the situation closely. Faraday's men fought back, but the police were prepared.

"Keep your eyes open for Lincoln!" Eli urged, his voice tense. "He could be here!"

Just as he spoke, he spotted a familiar figure trying to slip away through the shadows. "There he is! That's Lincoln!" Eli shouted.

"Should we alert Daniels?" Cole asked, anxiety creeping into his voice.

"Not yet. We need to see where he's going," Eli replied, his heart racing as he focused on the unfolding scene.

Lincoln ducked behind a stack of containers, trying to evade capture. Eli could feel the urgency building within him. They had to stop him before he got away.

"Come on, we need to help!" Eli insisted, opening the door of the van.

"Eli, wait!" Emma warned, but he was already moving.

**A Reckoning**

Eli sprinted toward the containers, determined to confront Lincoln. He rounded a corner just in time to see Lincoln pulling out a weapon, his expression twisted with anger.

"You think you can stop me?" Lincoln snarled, aiming the gun in Eli's direction.

Before Eli could react, a flash of movement caught his eye. Cole charged in, tackling Lincoln to the ground. The weapon skidded away, and a scuffle ensued.

"Eli, help!" Cole yelled as he wrestled with Lincoln.

Eli lunged forward, grabbing Lincoln by the shoulders and pulling him away from Cole. "You're finished, Lincoln!"

With a swift move, Eli pinned Lincoln down, adrenaline fueling his strength.

Just then, Daniels and a few officers arrived, quickly securing Lincoln.

"Nice work," Daniels said, panting slightly. "You two really took a risk."

Eli felt a wave of relief wash over him as they cuffed Lincoln. "We couldn't let him get away. Not after everything he's done."

**Aftermath and Reflection**

As dawn broke over the shipping yard, Eli and his friends watched as Lincoln and his remaining men were taken into custody. The weight of the night's events began to settle in.

"We did it," Emma said, her voice filled with disbelief. "We really did it."

Eli nodded, his heart swelling with pride. "We took a stand, and it mattered."

With the sun rising, the officers began to gather evidence and process the scene. Eli felt a renewed sense of purpose, knowing they had made a difference.

"Now, we just need to make sure this doesn't happen again," Carrie said, glancing at the police. "There's still work to be done."

"Agreed," Cole replied, determination etched on his face. "But at least we know we can fight back."

As they walked back toward the van, Eli couldn't shake the feeling of gratitude for his friends. They had faced danger together and emerged stronger.

In that moment, Eli realized they were no longer just kids caught in a terrifying situation—they were a team, ready to take on whatever challenges lay ahead.

# Chapter 23: A New Beginning

In the weeks that followed the raid, Eli and his friends witnessed the repercussions of their actions. Lincoln's operation was dismantled, and the network of criminals behind it was brought to justice. The community slowly began to heal from the chaos that had engulfed it.

Eli received calls from Officer Daniels, updating him on the investigation. "Your involvement was crucial, Eli. We couldn't have done this without you and your friends," Daniels said during one call.

"Thanks, but it was a team effort," Eli replied, pride swelling within him.

At school, the atmosphere shifted. Students felt safer, and the administration worked to implement programs aimed at prevention and awareness. Eli and his friends were invited to speak at a school assembly about their experiences.

As they stood before their classmates, Eli felt a rush of emotions. "We're all capable of making a difference," he said, looking out at the sea of faces. "It doesn't matter how old you are; standing up for what's right is what truly counts."

After the assembly, they received countless messages of support. Their bravery inspired others to share their stories, and a newfound sense of community emerged.

### Moving Forward

With summer approaching, Eli and his friends began to envision what lay ahead. They spent time together, not just as a team facing danger but as friends enjoying life.

One sunny afternoon, they gathered at a local park, laughing and sharing stories.

"Can you believe how far we've come?" Emma said, tossing a frisbee to Cole.

"It's crazy," Cole replied, catching it effortlessly. "I mean, we went from being targets to being heroes."

"Let's keep it going," Carrie suggested, a mischievous grin on her face. "We should start a community club—something that empowers others to stand up against bullying and crime."

Eli's heart swelled with pride at the thought. "That's an amazing idea. We could organize events, workshops, everything!"

As they tossed around ideas, Eli realized how far they had come. They had faced darkness together, and now they were stepping into the light, ready to make a lasting impact.

### A Bright Future

The sun began to set, casting a golden hue over the park. Eli looked around at his friends, their laughter filling the air.

No longer haunted by fear, they had transformed their experiences into strength and resolve.

"Here's to new beginnings," Eli said, raising an imaginary toast.

"To new beginnings!" his friends echoed, their voices ringing with hope.

As they watched the sunset, Eli felt a sense of peace wash over him. They had fought for what was right and emerged victorious.

The future lay before them, bright and full of possibilities, and they were ready to face it together.

# Chapter 24: A Legacy of Courage

As the summer sun shone down on the park, Eli and his friends gathered for the launch of their community club, aptly named "Voices of Change." They had spent weeks planning and preparing, eager to empower their peers and promote a culture of courage and resilience.

The day of the event arrived, and the park was bustling with energy. Colorful banners hung from trees, and tables were set up for various activities—workshops, informational booths, and even a resource table with information on reporting crime and seeking help.

Eli stood at the front, scanning the crowd. It felt surreal to see so many people coming together, united by a common purpose.

"Are you ready?" Emma asked, adjusting the microphone in her hand.

"More than ever," Eli replied, his heart racing with anticipation.

As they began the event, Eli welcomed everyone, sharing their story and the importance of standing up for what's right. The crowd listened intently, and Eli could see the impact of their words taking root.

"Together, we can create a safer community," Eli said passionately. "It starts with each of us being brave enough to speak out and support one another."

The crowd erupted in applause, and Eli felt a swell of pride. This was more than just a club; it was a movement, a legacy of courage that they were building together.

### Connecting with the Community

Throughout the day, workshops were held on topics like conflict resolution, self-defense, and how to identify and report suspicious behavior. Eli and his friends moved from station to station, engaging with attendees and sharing their knowledge.

Carrie led a workshop on conflict resolution, using role-playing exercises to demonstrate effective communication techniques. Cole taught self-defense moves, his enthusiasm infectious as he demonstrated basic techniques.

Eli roamed the park, witnessing the positive energy that filled the air. He saw students discussing their own experiences, forming connections, and encouraging each other to be active participants in their community.

As the sun began to set, Eli gathered everyone for a closing circle. They stood in a large circle, each person holding hands, a sense of unity enveloping them.

"I want everyone to share one thing they've learned today or how they plan to take action in our community," Eli said, his heart swelling with hope.

One by one, people spoke up—sharing stories of personal experiences, insights they gained from the workshops, and commitments to support one another. Eli listened, feeling the power of their shared resolve.

### Looking Ahead

As the event came to a close, Eli felt a sense of accomplishment wash over him. They had started something meaningful, and it was just the beginning.

"I can't believe how well this went," Emma said, her eyes sparkling. "We actually did it!"

"Yeah, and it was just the first step," Carrie added. "We can keep this going, hold more events, and reach even more people."

Eli smiled, looking at his friends. "This is about more than just today. It's about building a culture of courage that lasts."

As they packed up the supplies, Eli caught a glimpse of Lincoln's face in his mind. He remembered the fear and chaos they had faced, but it was overshadowed by the hope and unity they had created.

"I'm proud of us," Eli said, a sense of gratitude filling his heart. "We turned our pain into purpose."

**A New Chapter**

In the following weeks, "Voices of Change" continued to thrive. The club held regular meetings, organized events, and even partnered with local law enforcement to create safety workshops for the community.

Eli, Emma, Carrie, and Cole became leaders, not just in their club but in their community, inspiring others to stand up and take action. They built a network of support, where voices were heard, and change was possible.

As summer transitioned into fall, Eli reflected on how far they had come. Their experiences had transformed them, shaping them into advocates for change. The bonds of friendship they had forged during the darkest of times were now their greatest strength.

One afternoon, as they stood together at the park watching the leaves fall, Eli felt a sense of peace.

"Whatever comes next, we face it together," he said, looking at each of his friends.

"Together," they echoed, their voices filled with determination.

With renewed purpose, Eli and his friends stepped into the future, ready to face new challenges and make a difference. They had discovered the power of their voices and the strength of their unity, and they were determined to leave a lasting legacy—a legacy of courage, hope, and change.

The End !

==============================

**Disclaimer**

This novel is a work of fiction. While inspired by real-life events and issues, any resemblance to actual persons, living or dead, or actual events is purely coincidental. The characters, incidents, and dialogue are products of the author's imagination and are intended for entertainment purposes only. The themes explored within this story reflect societal challenges and the importance of courage, community, and resilience. Readers are encouraged to seek help and support in their own lives when facing adversity.

# About the Publisher

"**Knowledge is the most powerful tool for change.**" — Dr. Raam Harvard

At Poverty Eradication Trust (Triple ISO), we believe in the transformative power of knowledge. Founded with a mission to remove poverty from the world, foster education and inspire positive change, our publishing journey began with a vision to provide valuable resources that empower individuals and communities alike.

With several influential titles to our name, we have dedicated ourselves to curating a diverse range of books that address pressing issues, advance academic discourse, and offer practical solutions to global challenges. Each publication reflects our commitment to quality and our passion for making a meaningful impact.

Our books span a variety of fields, including psychology, social sciences, economics, and more. By partnering with esteemed authors and experts, we bring forward cutting-edge insights and practical tools designed to enrich the minds of students, professionals, and lifelong learners.

From university classrooms to community libraries, our titles are crafted to ignite curiosity, drive scholarly research, and support educational advancement. At Poverty Eradication Trust, we are more than just a publisher; we are advocates for change, dedicated to empowering our readers with the knowledge they need to make a difference in their world.

Join us on this journey of discovery and empowerment.

Explore our catalog and find the resources that will inspire your path to growth and success.

*DrRaam.com*